# Advance Praise for Catch Me When I Fall

"From the opening scene, *Catch Me When I Fall* will have readers rooting for the plucky heroine, as she walks across the narrow railing of the Kinsie Avenue River Bridge, thirty feet above the water. Intrepid, twelve-year-old Emma Monroe has two great desires. To discover the identity of her father. And to join a circus. Her mother ignores the first, and forbids the second. But determined and stubborn, Emma stares down each and every difficulty that stands in her way in the course of her quest for both. This is historical fiction at its very best. The depiction of life in the mid-west during the Great Depression is authentic in every detail, as is the portrayal of circus life in its heyday. Highly recommended."

- Janet Graber, McKnight Artist Fellow, is an award winning author. Her works include *Muktar and the Camels*, *The White Witch* and *Resistance*.

"The Big Top! Elephants! Trapeze artists! The sawdust swirls through this enchanting read by Bonnie Graves, catching young readers up into a thrilling world gone by, filled with sights, sounds, colors, and scents that convince them that indeed, they are there, under the Big Top in 1932, in the midst of the Depression, in Racine, Wisconsin, hitching a ride along with Emma, a lovable, spunky twelve year old. This delightful story of Emma Monroe, determined to find the identity of her father, will hook readers from the beginning chapter."

- Margo Sorenson, author of *Secrets in Translation*, finalist for the Minnesota Book Award in YA Fiction.

# CATCH ME WHEN I FALL

Bonnie Graves

Fitzroy Books

Published by Fitzroy Books, an imprint of
Regal House Publishing, in 2019
Regal House Publishing, LLC
Raleigh, NC 27612

Printed in the United States of America

ISBN -13: 978-1-947548-30-5
ISBN -13 (hardcover): 978-1-947548-01-5
ISBN -13 (epub): 978-1-947548-31-2
Library of Congress Control Number: 2018951820

Cover art © 2019 by C. B. Royal
Interior design by Lafayette & Greene
Cover design 2019 by Lafayette & Greene,
lafayetteandgreene.com

Fitzroy Books
fitzroybooks.com
Regal House Publishing, LLC
https://regalhousepublishing.com

For Mike, the love of my life.

# CHAPTER ONE

## SHOCK!

*Racine, Wisconsin, 1932*

Emma was concentrating on only one thing that hot July day—the Kinsie Avenue River Bridge just ahead of her, its narrow railing high above the river, the railing she bragged to Clarence she could walk. Her dog Lucky loped beside her, and her younger cousin Teddy ran just behind, trying to keep up.

"You're such a show off!" Clarence hollered. He was several yards behind them now on the road leading to the bridge. "You'll fall into the river and drown! Grow up!"

"Can't hear you!" Emma yelled back at her bossy older cousin and kept running toward the bridge. But the truth of it was she didn't feel as brave as she had just a few minutes ago. The water under the bridge wasn't swift and it wasn't deep, but it was a good thirty feet from the bridge railing to the muddy brown water of the Root River. Falling meant… well, she didn't want to think what it meant.

When they reached the bridge, Teddy tugged on her sleeve. "Don't…listen…to that dumb old Clarence," he said, trying to catch his breath. "Do it. I know you can."

"Of course I can." Emma put on her "I-can-do-this" face for her nine-year-old cousin. "And I will," she said, climbing up on the railing. The river looked a long way below her

1

now and smelled like rotting catfish, as it often did on hot summer days. The smell alone gave her reason not to fall. Other kids had fallen into the river trying to walk the railing. One had even drowned.

She stood holding the lamppost at the start of the bridge railing but didn't turn around to see if Clarence was watching. Instead she studied the sparkles on the river, like tiny explosions of stars. The hot cement railing prickled the soles of her bare feet. Now was her chance. She could do it. She *would* do it!

Emma took one hand off the lamppost and slowly found her balance on the narrow railing. Then she let go. She lifted her arms out, pretending she was a tightrope walker, like the ones on the circus billboard plastered across one whole side of Swensen's Bait and Tackle shack across the river. She focused on that billboard, slowly finding her balance on her front foot before she lifted her back foot and placed it forward, one sure step at a time.

Emma was nearly halfway across when she heard a motor car rumbling toward the bridge. "Hey!" someone shouted from the Model-T. And then a loud *honk, honk, honk*.

She felt herself losing her balance, leaning too far to the river side. She held steady on her front foot, her back foot wobbling in midair, her arms trying to keep herself from falling.

*Concentrate!* Emma commanded herself, staring at the billboard on the other side of the river. *You can do it.*

Right foot, left foot, right foot, left foot. She was almost there, almost to the lamppost. She reached out for it.

"Woo-hoo!" Teddy shouted when she grabbed the post.

Lucky barked.

She'd done it! Walked the entire Kinzie Avenue Bridge railing like a tightrope walker! Emma jumped down onto the bridge and threw her arms around Lucky. "I did it, boy." Lucky panted, his long, pink tongue lolling, his tail thwacking the road. Then she looked around for Clarence. She couldn't wait to see his face. But her cousin was nowhere in sight, the stinking coward.

"Now, I'm going to try!" Teddy said, climbing onto the railing.

"No!" Emma grabbed him and pulled him down.

"Hey!" he yelled. "Why'd you do that?"

"'Cause, dummy," Emma said. "You've got to do a hundred fence rails—without falling—before you try the bridge railing. Promise?"

"Aw, phooey."

"Promise?"

Teddy shoved his hands in his trouser pockets and kicked his bare feet on the bridge. "Oh, I guess."

"Promise you won't tell Mother? What I did?"

"Heck, I'm no snitch." Teddy gazed at the circus billboard. "So, want to join the circus? Bet you could."

Lucky chased after a huge black crow that had swooped down to peck at something in the road. The crow flapped up to the highest branches of a gnarled oak tree, cawed three times, and flew off.

"You could run away with the circus," Teddy said, as if running away were like running down to Brosky's for a loaf of bread.

"You're looney," Emma said, jogging back across the bridge, on the sidewalk this time. She could imagine a lot of things, but she couldn't imagine running away, even though Mother was so busy working at Dr. Rose's and doing other folks' laundry that she probably wouldn't even notice Emma was gone.

"Wish . . . we could go . . . to the circus tomorrow," Teddy said, running hard to keep up with her.

"Where would we get the fifty cents?" Emma kept going, heading toward College Avenue and her best friend's house.

At State Street, Emma halted to let Farmer Jensen's vegetable wagon pass. He tipped his hat at her. She waved back as Farmer Jensen's mule clomped down the street pulling the wagon behind him. Poor mule, she thought. What a load he had to bear in this heat.

"Besides," Emma said, running across State Street. "Mother won't let us go near the circus."

"Why?" Teddy asked.

"Don't know. She won't say."

"Just like she won't talk about your pa?"

"Shut up, Teddy. It's none of your beeswax." But Teddy was right. Mother never talked about Emma's father. And Emma dared not ask. It was a topic as forbidden as the apple God forbade Adam and Eve to eat. And the consequences to Emma seemed just as horrifying. "I'm going to Nan's now," she told Teddy. "Why don't you go play with Billy?"

"Aw, shucks. He's no fun."

"Then go find Clarence! He's a barrel of laughs! Ha, ha,

ha!" She raced away from Teddy, leaving him stranded on the corner with his mouth hanging open.

Emma might be rid of Teddy, but what he'd said about her "pa," gnawed at her. Who was her father anyway and why did no one ever talk about him? Had he done something horrible, too horrible to mention, or even think of? It didn't seem possible. Last summer, she had found a photograph hidden in a box in her mother's bureau, a photograph she suspected might be of her father. Why else would Mother hide it? The man in the photograph was too handsome to be an out-and-out criminal, or worse, a murderer. He had dark hair, dark eyes, and teeth as white as Clark Gable's. On the photograph was written: *To my sweet baby girl, with all my love, Papa.* Who else could this man be but her very own papa? Looking at that photo made Emma's imagination whirl with possibilities about who her father was. But one thing was certain. He was someone who loved her and someday she would find him.

When Emma got close to Tittle Brothers' Butcher Shop on Main Street, Lucky loped ahead of her. In summer, Mr. Tittle, like many other shop owners, always left a bowl of water on the sidewalk for thirsty dogs. After Lucky had licked the bowl dry, he stuck his nose in the open door, his tail wagging hopefully. On Saturdays, Mr. Tittle usually had a bone or two for Lucky. "You big, silly dog," Emma said, scratching behind his long, silky ears. "Today's only Friday. Sorry." He looked up at her with sorrowful brown eyes.

Lucky wasn't the only one in Racine looking for a handout that day. At least fifty men stood in the bread line in front of St. Joseph's, fanning their faces with caps or newspapers or whatever they had to stir up some air. A sadness seeped into Emma's bones as she watched these men across the street, dressed as if they hoped a job was in their future when all they were likely to get was some thin soup and stale bread—if they were lucky. Why didn't President Hoover do something? Emma knew what hunger felt like and was thankful Mother was one of the lucky ones who had a job. Emma didn't know how much money Mother earned taking in laundry and keeping house for Dr. Rose, but after he had hired Mother there had always been food on the table. Never quite enough food, though, for her two hungry cousins, or quite enough money for store-bought dresses for Emma.

As Emma reached Main Street another crow swooped from the rooftop of Hommel's Five and Dime and alighted on the sidewalk in front of Brosky's Market, cocking its head. Lucky chased after it. *Caw, caw, caw!* the crow scolded, flapping its shiny black wings until it found a safe perch on a nearby lamppost.

At Brosky's, Emma stared through the window at a circus poster taped to the glass. It was a picture of a man on a trapeze. Above the picture, she read, *Filippo the Flying Wonder.*

As she leaned in close to get a good look, she nearly wet her drawers. The man in the poster was the spitting image of the man in her mother's photograph, the man she suspected was her father! She had to get that photograph from her mother's bureau—she had to show Nan both the poster and the photograph.

# CHAPTER TWO

## THE PLAN

With the photograph now tucked safely between the pages of her new Nancy Drew book, Emma ran so fast across Main Street that she didn't see the streetcar.

Brakes screeched. Dust flew.

"You lookin' to get yourself killed, girlie?" the driver shouted, waving his fist at her.

"Sorry . . ." she gasped breathlessly.

Holy cow! How could she think about streetcars after what she had seen in Brosky's window? The man in the circus poster could be her very own father! The thought of it sent chills through her. Lucky ran next to her down the sidewalk toward Nan's house. Her best friend was the only person she could tell.

When Emma finally saw the Reiners' house on College Avenue, there sat Nan on her front porch swing—just as if this were any normal summer day. In front of the porch and up and down the walk, Mrs. Reiner's rosebushes exploded in a rainbow of colors.

"You won't believe what I just saw!" Emma called as she raced up the front walk.

Nan glanced up from her movie star magazine, her dark brown hair freshly cut in a stylish bob. "What?" A grin spread across Nan's face as Emma flew up the porch steps. "Clark

Gable and Greta Garbo smooching on Main Street?"

"More shocking than that!" Emma plopped down on the porch swing, her heart still racing, the book with the secret photograph resting on her lap, the bottom of her chambray shorts damp with perspiration.

"Oh, I know!" Nan said, her brown eyes wide. The swing stopped squeaking and Nan leaned close and whispered, "Dr. Rose kissing your mother. . .on the lips?" Emma got a whiff of lilac eau d'cologne. Nan giggled.

"Cut it out! That's not funny. Come with me to Brosky's. You've got to see this with your own eyes."

Nan glanced at the book on Emma's lap. "Oh, *The Hidden Staircase*! I love Nancy Drew. Can I borrow that when you're done?"

"It's a library book," Emma said, not yet giving away the secret of what lay hidden between the pages. Emma grabbed Nan's hand and pulled her off the porch swing. "Let's go!"

"This better be good! It's hotter than blazes. Sometimes, Emma, you're such a tomboy! Bare feet! Honestly!" Nan, on the other hand, was no tomboy. She looked more like someone out of the Sears Catalog in her blue cotton sundress with drop waist, white patent leather shoes and ankle socks. Nan opened the screen door and stuck her head in. "Mama, I'm going downtown with Emma!"

"All right, darling," Mrs. Reiner called. "I'll make some lemonade for when you girls get back. Don't get overheated, now. Wear your hat!"

Nan snatched her straw cloche off the hook and pressed it on her head like a helmet. "I wouldn't be moving from that porch swing if you weren't my very best friend!"

Emma hurried with Nan back to Main Street, Lucky keeping pace with them.

"Look at that!" Emma said, when they reached Brosky's Market. She pointed at the circus poster while Lucky noisily lapped up all the water in the bowl left by the door.

"You dragged me all the way here to show me that?" Nan asked, hands on her hips. "We know the circus is coming tomorrow. So what? You know you can't go."

"No, look at *him*," Emma insisted, pointing to the picture of the man on the flying trapeze, Filippo the Flying Wonder. "I think he's—" She glanced around to make sure no one was listening and cupped her hands around Nan's ear. "—my…father!" She could hardly say the word.

"What? You've never seen your father!"

"Remember the photograph I showed you? The one hidden in Mother's bureau?"

"The handsome man you *think* is your father?"

Emma opened *The Hidden Staircase* and pulled out the photograph, holding it out for Nan to inspect. "Take a good look at this."

Nan peered at the photograph and then at the poster.

"See," Emma said. "He has exactly the same wavy dark hair parted on the side. And look at his chin!" Emma stuck out her own chin. "Look at that dimple. Just like mine. Just like this!" Emma jabbed her finger at the man's dimple in the photograph. "And the eyes. I've memorized the man's eyes. They look the same as Filippo the Flying Wonder's." Emma's heart raced.

The iceman's truck pulled up to the curb. Emma and Nan stared at the huge, shirtless man in overalls as he carried an enormous block of ice on his shoulder into Brosky's.

"Don't you see?" Emma said more softly, looking around to make sure no one was watching them. "Now's my chance. . .tomorrow at the circus. I'm going to find out if this man could really be—my . . . *father.*" Emma tore the poster off the window, rolled it up into a narrow cylinder and stuck it down her back, between her blouse and undershirt.

Nan stared at her bug-eyed. "Emma! Honestly! What are you going to do with that?"

"Keep it."

"Okay. But then what? How do you plan to find this Filippo guy? And besides, what if that photograph isn't your mother's? Maybe she's saving it for someone else. Maybe it's not your father. Why don't you just ask her?"

"Are you kidding? If she knew I was snooping in her bureau, she'd whup me good. You know she won't talk about my father." When Emma was little, she thought Mother might have plucked her out of a basket floating in the river, like baby Moses. Then she found the photograph in the drawer and began to put two and two together. And now, here was Filippo the Flying Wonder who looked so much like the man in the photograph! He truly *could* be her father. Why else would Mother have that photograph in her bureau? Emma had to find out the truth, and now was her chance. Except she had little time. The poster said there was only one performance—tomorrow afternoon at two. The circus would be setting up before dawn tomorrow and leaving after The Big Show.

"So, what are you going to do?" Nan asked.

"Help set up the circus like Eddie Glover and Hank Swensen did last summer. That way, I can look around. Meet the circus people and find Filippo the Flying Wonder. If I work hard enough, I can earn a ticket to the Big Show and see him."

A shadow fell across the sidewalk. Emma felt a yank on her braid.

"So, I see you didn't drown," Clarence said, his ginger hair a mess of sweaty tangles, his abundant freckles glistening in the hot sun.

"Didn't fall either. Walked the whole bridge railing." Emma lifted her chin, at the same time hiding the book that held the secret photograph behind her and out of Clarence's view.

"Yah, I bet."

"Just ask Teddy." Emma suspected Clarence had stayed to watch her, hidden somewhere out of sight. Just didn't want to admit it.

"He'd lie for you any day, and you know it. What's this about the circus, anyway?" Clarence asked.

"Emma is going to work to earn a ticket," Nan said. "Like Eddie and Hank did last summer."

Emma pressed down hard on Nan's patent leather shoe with her bare foot.

"Emma Monroe, a circus roustabout. Ain't that the funniest thing I ever heard?" Clarence threw his head back and howled.

Emma felt that urge to let loose the temper Mother said she had to tame. She jabbed Clarence's ribs with her elbow, and said fiercely, "I *am* going to get a job at the circus grounds!" She jutted out her chin. "I am."

11

"Yeah? Like heck you are." Clarence pushed Emma's shoulder. Lucky, who sat panting in a narrow slice of shade close to the building, barked. "You could never get a job setting up the circus. Girls ain't allowed. It's a man's work." Clarence grinned, flexing his measly arms. Two poor excuses for muscles sprouted like cherry pits under his baby pink skin. His freckled face beaded up with even more sweat in the noonday sun. While Clarence's eyes were shut under the strain of his muscular prowess, Emma handed Nan the Nancy Drew book with the photograph.

"That's nothing. Look at these!" Emma bent her elbows, clenched her fists, and pumped up two muscles of her own, bigger than Clarence's, even though he was a boy and fourteen, two whole years older than Emma. But Emma could chin herself twenty times, do backwards flips, climb a flagpole, and walk across the Kinzie Avenue Bridge railing! All sorts of tricks that Clarence could only dream of doing.

"That's nothin'," Clarence said, dismissing her with a flick of his hand. "Takes more than a couple muscles to get a job at the circus."

"Like being smart and working hard?" Emma asked.

"Yep."

"Smartest thing I ever heard you say, Clarence Sissy Johnson!"

Emma grabbed Nan's hand and ran down the sidewalk, leaving Clarence to consider his new middle name. Tomorrow, she was going to the circus to find the man who might truly be her father...*if* Clarence didn't tattle to Mother about her plans and ruin everything before she had the chance.

12

# CHAPTER THREE

## LIES AND SECRETS

Emma!" Mother scolded, as Emma raced into the kitchen,
Lucky's toenails clickety-clicking on the linoleum floor
behind her. "You forgot again! Look at that mess!" Mother
pointed to the water pooling underneath the icebox. It was
Emma's daily job to empty the pan that held the water from
the melting block of ice.

"Sorry. I'll clean it up." Emma lay the yellow roses on the
counter, the ones she had carefully selected for Mother from
Mrs. Reiner's garden, and pulled her apron off the hook.

"What were you so busy doing that you forgot again?"
Mother asked, without turning around. She stood at the sink,
her wavy auburn hair falling around her slender shoulders,
wearing the same faded wash dress she had on yesterday.
The ties on her apron dangled limply, as if she couldn't be
bothered to tie a bow.

Emma ignored Mother's question. The truth was she had
stayed too long at Nan's drinking lemonade, listening to Mrs.
Reiner's gossip, and snipping the roses for Mother's bouquet.
Someday, she hoped, Mother would have time to sit down
and talk with her like Mrs. Reiner did, not just ask prying
questions and tell her things to do or not to do.

Emma grabbed the rag mop and bucket from the closet
and began sopping up the water.

"You didn't do that basket of Mrs. Olsen's laundry either."

"No. I don't remember you telling me." Emma wrung out the mop with her bare hands. The brownish water reminded her of the river, of her balancing act on the Kinzie Avenue Bridge railing. But instead of rotting catfish, the bucket water smelled of spoiled food. What would Mother do if she knew Emma had run around barefoot all day, much less walked across the Kinzie Avenue Bridge railing? At least she had remembered to collect her worn-out shoes from her secret hiding place—the hollow in the tree by the lake—and put them on before she walked in the house. She had also stashed the circus poster and the Nancy Drew book in the tree hollow until she could safely sneak them home.

"Would you like me to do the laundry now?" Emma asked. She emptied the bucket, then filled a Mason jar with water, arranged the yellow roses in it, and set them on the window ledge. When would Mother notice them?

"The laundry's drying on the line," Mother told her.

Mrs. Olsen's laundry was just another chore Emma had forgotten to do. She didn't mean to. It's just that, well, more important things always seemed to get in the way of what she was supposed to do.

"It's time for supper. Wash your hands and set the table."

"It's Teddy's turn!"

"Is not!" Teddy yelled from somewhere.

"Is too!" Emma shouted.

"Not!"

"Stop it, you two. Get those hands washed and set the table, young lady. Right now."

Emma winced at the words "young lady." Did Mother

think she could turn her into one just by using the words?
Teddy had better remember his promise not to tattle about
the river bridge, or she would be in a lot more trouble. But
Clarence was right about Teddy. Teddy usually did stick up
for her. Not that stinking Clarence, though. He better not go
blabbing about the circus or she'd never have the chance to
find Filippo the Flying Wonder. The circus would be gone
soon after the matinee. Tomorrow was her one and only
chance to find out if Filippo was really her father.

On her way to the bathroom, Emma poked her head into
the parlor to see if Granddad was in his favorite chair. He
wasn't. Probably still at Dania where he liked to have his
schnapps and cigar.

The bathroom smelled like pee. Ever since her cousins
Clarence and Teddy had moved in— after Aunt Grace died,
and Uncle Pete lost his farm and had hopped the rails to
find work in California—pee had become a familiar odor,
especially on Fridays. It wasn't until Saturday that Mother
did house cleaning at *their* house. Every other day of the
week, except Sunday, she was keeping Dr. Rose's big house
overlooking Lake Michigan clean and free of unpleasant
smells—not their house. Emma grabbed the bar of Ivory
soap from the sink, working up a frothy lather. Her blisters
stung, punishment probably for those tricks she stopped to
do on the monkey bars after Nan's house instead of coming
home to help with the laundry. The truth of it was she didn't
remember Mother saying anything about the laundry.

The dirt under Emma's stubby fingernails refused to
budge. "So what?" she said out loud. Lucky's tail thump-

thumped on the bathroom floor. "Boys always have dirty fingernails," she told him. "And tomorrow I have to look like one!" Clarence was right about one thing. She knew the circus boss wouldn't let a girl work.

Emma stared at her face in the mirror. Freckles cascaded over her nose and spilled onto her red cheeks, now streaked with dirt. Damp curls had escaped from her pigtails and frizzed around her ears. She batted her long, brown eyelashes—her best feature, she had been told—those and her brown eyes that Granddad said were flecked with silver. "Sparks," Granddad called them. But hard as she looked, Emma could never see those sparks herself. One thing was certain, she wasn't beautiful, like Mother. Maybe someday. Still, she wasn't going to end up like Mother, cleaning other people's toilets and washing their underwear!

Emma leaned closer to the mirror. Could this face of hers pass for a boy's? It had to. Tomorrow she would tuck her hair into Granddad's old brown fedora, wear Clarence's outgrown boots and overalls. She stuck her tongue out at her reflection. "That's what you get for trying to pass yourself off for a dumb boy," she scolded herself in the mirror. But it was her only hope.

When she walked back into the kitchen, Mother was hovering over the stove, pouring green beans into a pot. Steam rose up, adding more heat to the already hot, sticky kitchen.

The screen door slammed and in sauntered Clarence carrying a bucket. "Here, Aunt Saffy," he said, showing her the bucket filled with raspberries, his face beaming like he'd brought her a pot of gold. Seeing that bucket filled with luscious red berries made Emma wish she'd been the one who had spotted the raspberry bushes.

Mother smiled at Clarence. "Thank you. They look delicious. Set the bucket in the sink for now."

Emma glanced at the bouquet on the window ledge. "Mother, do you like the roses? They're your favorite color."

"They're lovely," Mother said. "Where did they come from?"

"Mrs. Reiner's rose garden." The roses didn't look as happy as they did in Mrs. Reiner's garden. Emma probably shouldn't have stopped at the monkey bars and left them without water for so long.

Clarence set the bucket of raspberries in the sink while Emma pulled open the silverware drawer. "Don't you dare say anything about the bridge or the circus," Emma whispered to him.

Lucky lapped noisily at his water bowl, his long tail swishing against her bare leg.

"I'll have to remember to thank Mrs. Reiner," Mother said.

Emma plunked a knife and fork at Mother's place on the table. *What about me?* Emma wanted to yell. *The bouquet was my idea.*

"Go wash for dinner, Clarence."

As Clarence passed Emma, he bumped her with his bony shoulder. "You owe me!"

"PU!" Emma pinched her nose shut. Clarence smelled of body odor like always. Maybe for Christmas she would give him a bar of Lifebuoy soap. He gave her his I'm-so-much-better-than-you smirk and shook his head.

"What?" she asked.

"You know," he whispered all snarly.

Emma glared at Clarence.

"Teddy!" Mother called. "Have you washed?"

"Are we eating without Granddad?" Emma asked.

"I think he's helping out at Dania tonight," Mother told her.

When they sat down at the table, their hands washed, Mother said grace. Emma couldn't wait to bite into her juicy hamburger. She was famished.

As soon as they chimed in with "Amen," Emma picked up her hamburger, bit down, and began to chew. Something didn't taste right. She knew right away this wasn't a *hamburger*.

"Aunt Saffy," Teddy said, lifting the top bun and stabbing the lettuce and pickle with his fork. "There ain't no meat! Only pickles and lettuce!"

"Hooverburgers again," Emma grumbled.

"It was either hamburger or milk," Mother said. "You'll have milk with your oatmeal tomorrow. Be thankful for that."

"And raspberries," said Clarence, who looked at his empty plate like he was about to cry. Already he'd devoured his Hooverburger and most of his green beans and potato salad. Besides having BO, Clarence was always hungry and still skinny as a flagpole.

Emma's gaze drifted to the yellow roses and then out the kitchen window to the laundry on the line—brassieres, skivvies, and what-have-you's—none of it theirs. She hated the thought of Mother washing other folks' underwear. She should help her more, but she hated the thought of other folks' undies worse. She despised the smell of bleach and how it stung her eyes. She guessed she was a bad person to have these thoughts, to spend time fooling around instead of helping Mother. If Mother had a husband like Nan's mother did, would she have to take in laundry? Emma's thoughts drifted to Filippo the Flying Wonder. Her stomach fluttered with the possibility that this man might be her very own father, a famous circus performer! Was he? And if he was, why didn't he live with them—and why did Mother keep him a deep dark secret? Would she find out tomorrow?

Mother got up and switched on the radio. They ate in silence listening to Kate Smith warble, until the WGN announcer reminded listeners about Hackenstack's Most Spectacular Show on Earth tomorrow. Emma's heart skipped a beat.

"Can we go, Aunt Saffy? Please? Can we? Can we?" Teddy begged.

Mother didn't answer. But she didn't have to. Her look said everything.

Teddy's eyes filled with tears.

Emma's heart did break a little for poor Teddy.

The back door creaked open and Granddad strolled in bringing the familiar smell of cigar smoke with him. "Sorry I'm late," he said, taking off his straw bowler hat and hanging it on the hat rack. He wiped his forehead with the back of his hand. "I ran into Dr. Rose making a call at the Stovers."

"Everything all right?" Mother asked.

"Oh, fine. Little Nellie just stuck a few peas in her ear

again. I swear. I think that child must mistake her ear for her mouth."

"She probably doesn't want to eat her peas and is hiding them in her ear!" Teddy called.

"Now there's a thought," Granddad said, sitting down at his place at the end of the table. "Someone ought to pass that insight along to Mrs. Stover."

Mother got up to fix Granddad's plate. Granddad was a tall man, but sitting in the kitchen chair you wouldn't know it. He had a long nose and wore glasses that were often smudged. But his eyes were a deep blue like the water in the quarry, and he smiled a lot, which made his eyes twinkle.

"We're having Hooverburgers," Teddy told him.

"My favorite," Granddad said, winking at Emma, his eyes sparkling behind his smudged glasses.

"They ain't got meat," Teddy said.

"They don't have meat," Mother corrected, big on grammar and proper language since she had started working for Dr. Rose. Emma thought again about what Nan had said earlier that day—Mother kissing Dr. Rose—and felt herself blushing.

Granddad looked over at Emma and smiled. Could he read her thoughts? She sometimes thought he could. "Hamburger is a luxury these days," Granddad said. "We must be grateful for what we have. As long as I have a cigar, I can do without meat, thank you."

Granddad smiled at Emma as Mother handed him a plate with a Hooverburger, a few green beans and a dollop of potato salad, probably the last of it.

Clarence glanced all droopy-faced at Granddad's plate. Emma knew as well as Clarence—no chance of second helpings.

"Did Aunt Saffy tell you children about Dr. Rose's Fourth of July party tomorrow?" Granddad asked. "We're all invited."

"Whoopee!" Teddy shouted. "Will there be fireworks?"

"Is it Fourth of July?" Granddad said, raising his fork like the Statue of Liberty torch.

"And food?" Clarence asked.

"Yes. Plenty," Mother said. "I placed the order at Brosky's yesterday."

"What time's the party?" Emma asked, squirming in her chair.

"Five o'clock," Mother answered.

Relief rippled through Emma. That would give her plenty of time to see the circus matinee, find Filippo the Flying Wonder, and get to the party before Mother suspected anything!

"Can we go to the circus matinee first, Aunt Saffy? Please?" Teddy asked again.

Mother and Granddad exchanged glances—glances that meant they knew something she and her cousins didn't. The color seemed to drain from Mother's face.

"Mother, what's the matter?" Emma asked.

"Nothing. I just…"

"Maybe you should try Lydia Pinkham's Vegetable Compound," Emma suggested.

Granddad snickered, spearing string beans on his fork.

"What?" Mother said.

"That's what Mrs. Reiner takes. She's always so lively and cheerful."

"I'd be more lively and cheerful if you spent less time playing and more time helping with chores," Mother said.

Emma stared down at her plate, embarrassed to be scolded in front of everyone. Her feet felt burning hot inside her too-small shoes. A weight like a stone seemed to settle on her heart.

"You know, Sapphira, I think the children should do their fair share of chores," Granddad said. "But they need to exercise their imaginations as well as their muscles. Emma, if you helped your mother more, perhaps she could take more time to play. Heaven knows she used to be the Queen of Play when she was your age, having no mother to supervise her. And I was too busy with work to pay much attention."

At Granddad's words, some of the heaviness lifted from Emma's heart. She decided now was the time to ask, before she lost her nerve, while Granddad was there to maybe take her side. She crossed her fingers behind her back. "Can I go early to the Reiners' tomorrow so Nan and me can help Mr. Reiner on his milk route?"

"Nan and I," Mother corrected.

"So, can I?"

"May I."

"So, may I?"

Clarence squinted his eyes at Emma—*You little liar*, they seemed to say.

"Well, I suppose," Mother said. "If you help fold and sort

the laundry before you go to bed."

"Of course, Mother. Sorry, I forgot."

"I'll be at Dr. Rose's all day tomorrow getting ready for the Fourth of July party. But you'll have to leave earlier than I do for the milk route."

"Can I go, too?" Teddy begged.

"No, Teddy," Emma said. "There's no room in the wagon."

"Phooey! Emma gets to have all the fun!"

"Can…may I stay for lunch if Mrs. Reiner asks me?"

"For heaven's sake, Emma, you spend half your days at the Reiners'."

"The Reiners like me," she said, thinking of the hugs, juicy gossip, and beauty tips she got from Mrs. Reiner, not that she used any of the tips herself.

"Well, don't make yourself a bother, and you and Nan stay away from the circus grounds. It's no place for girls."

"Yes, Mother."

"May I please be excused now?"

Mother nodded.

Emma picked up her dishes and nearly danced to the sink. She felt giddy with excitement. Her plan was working. Tomorrow she would earn her way into the circus and find Filippo the Flying Wonder—the man who very possibly could be her own father!

# Chapter Four

## No Turning Back

One important task was left for Emma that evening—retrieving the book with the photograph and the circus poster. The Jack Benny Radio Show came on eight o'clock. She knew her family would be tuned into that. It would be the perfect time to sneak out.

Just before eight o'clock, after she had the laundry neatly folded and set on Mother's bed, Emma peeked into the parlor. There they all gathered—Mother on the sofa with her mending, Granddad in his chair smoking his stub of a cigar, Clarence and Teddy sprawled on the floor. Even Lucky lay curled up next to Teddy, his head cocked toward the radio as if anticipating Mr. Jack Benny's jokes.

Should she say something? No, she decided. She wouldn't be missed.

The kitchen screen door squeaked when Emma opened it. She waited a minute, hoping no one heard, then shot down the walk and across the neighbor's lawn. There was no time to waste. She had less than thirty minutes.

The streets of Racine were strangely deserted for a summer night. A breeze from the lake cooled her face as she ran. Dogs, protecting their territory, barked at her. A few boys lit firecrackers on the sidewalk in front of their houses. The explosions, like gunshots, startled her and made her run even faster toward Lake Michigan.

Her secret hiding spot was a hollowed-out tree trunk just over a steep bank that led down to the lake. Bushes and tall weeds around the tree provided camoflage. She had found the hollow in the tree trunk a few weeks earlier when she threw a stick for Lucky to catch and it landed at the foot of the tree, almost as if meant to point her to it.

When she reached the bank and scrambled down to the tree, she was startled to see someone or something had trampled the weeds around it and parted the bushes. Had her treasures been found and taken? Her heart started pounding. She couldn't imagine what horrible fate lay in store for her if the photograph was gone. What would Mother think? Do? And the library book? Where would she find the money to pay for that?

The most awful feeling gnawed in Emma's stomach. She fell on her knees and dug into the hollow. Her sweaty hands grasped something. The book. It was there. Quickly she flipped opened the pages. The photograph! No one had taken it or the circus poster. Sweet relief welled up inside of Emma. All was well. For now, anyway. But she had to hurry. She had to get back before the Jack Benny Show ended.

Wedging the rolled-up circus poster against her back, between her blouse and undershirt, and clasping the book with the photograph, Emma ran the ten blocks back to her house. At the backdoor, she stopped to catch her breath and to listen. She heard laughter from the parlor. She was safe. At least for a few more minutes.

Emma tip-toed up to Mother's room across the hall from

her own, breathing in the familiar and comforting smell of Granddad's cigar. She yanked open the bureau drawer and, lifting Mother's carefully folded underwear, felt for the box. As she started to set the photograph back inside the box with the feathered headband, another thought came to her. Why put the photograph back? It could be proof. She could show it to one of the circus workers. *Is this Filippo the Flying Wonder?* she'd ask. And if they said "yes," she'd tell them . . . tell them what? At the sound of footsteps on the stairs, she quickly slipped the photograph back between the pages of the Nancy Drew book.

Clarence stood at the door like a sentry. "Why are you in Aunt Saffy's bedroom?"

"None of your beeswax," Emma replied, defiantly.

"You're up to something, aren't you, Emma? Something besides trying to get a job at the circus. I can smell it." The smirk on Clarence's face made Emma want to slap him.

She pushed by Clarence, holding her nose as she passed. "I smell you! PU! And you better keep your trap shut about the circus, or I'll—"

"You'll what? You'll what, Emma?" he said, tauntingly.

"I'll think of something!" She stomped across the hall to their bedroom, the one she, Clarence, and Teddy shared.

"Hey, what's that on your back? Stuck in your shirt?" he asked.

Once inside the bedroom, Emma slammed the door, hard. "Don't you dare come in! I'm getting undressed."

That Clarence. As if she didn't have enough to worry about. So far he had kept his word about not telling on her, but with Clarence, you could never be sure.

Lucky whined and pawed at the door. When she opened it, he jumped up on her. "I'm OK," she said. Satisfied with her answer, he made himself comfortable on her bed.

Emma lifted the circus poster out of her blouse and hid it behind her winter coat in the corner of her closet. Next, she pulled the photograph from between the pages of *The Hidden Staircase*. "Thanks for taking good care of my secret, Nancy," she whispered. Emma smiled at the thought of her hero, Nancy, guarding Emma's photograph. "Now, wish me luck." Emma tucked the photograph into the front pocket of Clarence's outgrown bib overalls, the overalls that hung in Emma's closet waiting for her to slip on at the crack of dawn. She hoped and prayed Mother wouldn't look for the photograph and find it missing.

"Time for bed, Emma!" Mother called from the bottom of the stairs.

"In a minute!" Emma yelled back.

They did that a lot lately, Mother and her, yelling back and forth from downstairs to upstairs. Tonight, Emma was glad of it. She couldn't be caught with the poster now, or the photograph.

Outside her window in the twilight, Clarence and Teddy sat on a stump in the backyard shooting at squirrels with their slingshots. They both had a bedtime later than hers. It wasn't fair, but that's the way it was with boys. They had all the freedom. At least it gave her some time to herself before they flung their smelly bodies onto the cots in the bedroom they all shared. Still, how she wished she were outside catching fireflies, or doing cartwheels, or swinging on the rope that hung from the big oak tree. It was hard to go to bed on these hot summer nights where twilight lingered well past her bedtime.

Emma gazed across the treetops, now dark silhouettes against the dusky sky, toward the south and Lake Michigan where the circus would be set up before sunrise tomorrow. It couldn't come soon enough.

As Emma undid her braids and slipped her nightgown over her head, the smell of the freshly laundered gown gave Emma a twinge of guilt for not helping with the laundry and for lying to Mother. Lying wasn't something Emma did often, unless it was important, and getting a circus ticket would be the most important thing she'd ever have done in her life.

She heard the bedroom door open. "I left some cookies on the kitchen table for you to take to the Reiners," Mother said. "Don't forget to take them."

"That was swell of you," Emma said. Mother rarely baked sweets for them. Sugar was a luxury, after all. "Emma suspected she must have baked them at Dr. Rose's."

"Well, it's the least I can do. You're there so much."

"Mrs. Reiner's nice." Emma didn't mention how much more fun Mrs. Reiner was than Mother, how she acted more like a friend than a mother. But Mother was prettier, which made Emma wonder if she really was her daughter. Nan had told her once that Mr. Reiner had called Mother a "looker who turned the head of every man in Racine." Emma could never turn any boy's head, not that she'd even want to. Have a boy stare at her? For what? She was as plain as a girl could be, except for her long eyelashes, and her wild, curly hair that she wore most of the time in braids.

"Be sure to thank her for the roses. And after lunch tomorrow, come straight over to Dr. Rose's. I'll need your help."

Emma felt her stomach tighten. The circus matinee started at two and probably lasted until four. And then Emma had to find and talk to Filippo. Would Clarence tell on her? Would Mother come to the circus looking for her? For now, she would just have to brush those horrifying thoughts aside. She wasn't about to let anything deter her.

Mother lingered in the doorway, looking at Emma as if she wanted to say something more. She wished Mother would come in and kiss her goodnight like she used to do when Emma was little. Did all mothers stop hugging and kissing when their daughters got to a certain age? No, not Nan's anyway. Emma wondered about fathers—if they hugged and kissed their daughters, too. She'd never thought about it much before, but now that she was about to meet her father, it was something to consider.

"Mother?"

"Yes?"

"Nothing...I mean, sleep well."

"You, too. And remember, I don't want you milling around that circus tomorrow."

"Yes, Mother." Emma's fingers crossed tightly behind her back.

୫୦

At the first crow of the rooster, Emma dressed without

making a sound. Even though Clarence's old overalls had been laundered, they still held a trace of his unpleasant body odor. Lucky sat on his haunches and cocked his head at her, wondering what they were doing up at this hour. Teddy took a sputtering breath, as if startled by a dream and, on the cot next to him, Clarence snored softly. At least he hadn't tattled on her—yet. There was barely enough light to make out Granddad's fedora and Clarence's old boots that she'd set on the closet floor. She grabbed the hat and boots and started for the stairs. The fear of being caught—and the thrill of escape—see-sawed inside her.

The wooden steps creaked, despite her careful tip-toeing. Lucky followed close behind. Emma felt her way through the dark kitchen, grabbing an apple from a bowl on the counter and the plate of cookies for the Reiners. The last thing she wanted to do was to wake Granddad who slept in the tiny room draped off from the parlor.

"Who's there?" Granddad asked.

Emma turned around quickly, her heart racing. Granddad was barely visible to her in the dark kitchen.

He flipped on the light.

"My goodness. I thought you were a boy in those overalls and . . . is that my hat?"

"It is Granddad. Your old one. The one you don't wear anymore. Do you mind?"

He scratched his head of gray hair. "Why would I?  It will look a heap better on you than it ever did on me." He laughed loudly.

Emma looked toward the stairs, expecting to see her

mother too. But thankfully, there was no sign of her. Emma had to get out soon, but Granddad kept talking.

"My," he said," but you do remind me of your mama at your age. A mind of her own, that girl, always up to something. So, tell me, Emma. What are *you* up to dressed like a boy?"

Emma swallowed hard and crossed her fingers behind her back. "Going with Nan and Mr. Reiner on his milk route. Remember? I've gotta run, Granddad, or I'll be late."

"Well, go ahead then, sweetheart. Skadattle!"

Emma breathed a sigh of relief as she escaped through the kitchen door, Lucky at her heels.

Outside, birds chirped noisily from hidden perches. Underfoot, the grass was heavy with dew, and the air smelled fresh and rich, like the whole world was ripe for the picking. Emma tied up her thick, wild curls with a rubber band and tucked them into Granddad's old brown fedora. As soon as every last curl was hidden, she started racing toward Nan's house.

In the predawn light, Emma could see Nan on the porch swing, exactly as they'd planned yesterday when Nan swore on the Bible she wouldn't tell on Emma.

Nan giggled when she saw Emma. "Honestly! You look just like a boy in those overalls and hat!"

"Shhh!" Emma whispered. "Has your father left on his route?"

"Ages ago. And Mother sleeps with a mask and plugs in her ears. A freight train couldn't wake her. Not until eight o'clock anyway. Beauty sleep, you know."

"Mother made these for you," Emma said, handing Nan the plate of cookies.

"Oh, how nice. Sugar cookies, my favorite."

"You'll take good care of Lucky?"

"Yum," Nan said, chomping on a cookie. "Of course, you silly!"

Emma knelt down beside Lucky and took his soft muzzle in her hands. She thought about the first day he'd come around their backdoor, a scraggly looking pup. Forgotten or discarded by someone. It took weeks of begging, of spiffing up that mutt, before she convinced Mother to let her keep him. "You be a good boy, now. I'll see you after the circus." Lucky licked Emma's cheek.

"Aren't you scared?" Nan asked.

"A little," Emma admitted, wiping her moist cheek with the back of her hand. "But I've got to do this. I've got to find the man on the poster, Filippo."

"You really think he's your father?"

"I do, Nan. I really do."

Something like fear or excitement—Emma couldn't decide which—rippled through her, like the feeling she got from swinging high on the rope over the Root River just before she let go.

# Chapter Five

## The Circus

Emma ran the five blocks from Nan's house to the parched field above Lake Michigan where the circus would be set up. Just as she reached Twenty-First Street, the streetlights flickered off and the sun slipped out of the water, throwing color into the sky—red and purple, and pink and gold. While the morning run got her heart pumping, the next sight nearly made it stop. Even brighter than the sunrise, parked on the railroad spur that came out of Case Tractor Works, sat the painted railroad cars of Hackenstack's Most Spectacular Show on Earth!

She held her breath, amazed at the sight before her—men were unloading red-and-gold-painted circus wagons from the flatcars; elephants were being led onto the circus lot, and the first tent was going up before her very eyes. She walked as close as she dared, just to the edge of the field, just close enough to breathe in the smells of animals and hay and sawdust, close enough to be filled with excited jitters.

At the far end of the field, near the circus wagons and flatcars, a tall man wearing a huge white cowboy hat bossed everyone around. "OK, get your back into it!" he yelled at the workers. No sooner had he said that than the second tent was up and men were leading animals into it—monkeys, parrots, and birds with feathers every color of the rainbow. Emma's heart beat fast. She was here—closer to the circus than she had ever dreamed possible. That afternoon, if she got good and lucky, she'd be sitting underneath the Big Top, watching the Big Show, waiting to see Filippo the Flying Wonder, the man she thought must be—had to be—her father.

As she walked farther onto the lot, trying to think how she was going to offer her services, the man with the cowboy hat yelled at her. "Hey, you! Rube! Where you think you're goin'?"

In a flash, she yelled back, "Need help?" Then quickly lowered her voice: "I'll do anything you want for a ticket to the show."

The man eyed her up and down. She didn't know whether to slouch like a dumb boy or stand taller. "I'm tougher than I look," she told him, pulling down the rim of Granddad's fedora. "I'm used to hard work. Can do twenty-five chin-ups." Twenty-five sounded better than twenty. What could it hurt to add a few more?

"Twenty-five chin-ups, eh? And I suppose you can do handstands and back flips, too."

"Yes, sir. Want me to show you?"

The man stood quiet for a spell, rubbing his chin. "You ain't thinking of joining the circus, are you?"

"No, sir. Just want to see the Most Spectacular Show on Earth, that's all." Her throat felt hoarse trying to keep her voice low.

"Well, then, see those elephants? See that hose over there? See that bucket? Fill that bucket with water and take it to the first elephant. Then get another bucket of water and take it

34

to the second elephant. Then get another bucket and fill it. Keep filling and carrying till them pachyderms don't want any more water. Get it?"

"Yes, sir!" Emma said. She wasn't used to saying "sir," but figured politeness would pay off.

"And kid, remember, those are wild animals. Respect that. When you're through, come and see me," the man said.

Wild animals? Emma stared at the huge elephants all in a row. Of course they were wild animals! Emma tingled all over at the thought of providing water for these giant— what did the man call them?—pachyderms. To think they had come all the way from India or Africa or other faraway lands. And she got to give them water! Her plan was working close to perfect. All she had to do was what the boss said and a ticket to the circus would be hers, easy as pie. Quickly she got the bucket, found the hose, filled the bucket, and carried it to the first elephant. Holy cow, was he enormous! Never in her life had she been so close to such a gigantic animal, its legs as huge as tree trunks. And now, nine of these giants, all in a row, towered above her, rocking back and forth. A canvas strap around one leg, tethered to a chain, kept them from running off.

Before she'd watered the second elephant, the first was ready for more, but he'd have to wait. There were seven more down the line. Back and forth, back and forth those elephants rocked. The motion made her dizzy, the work made her thirsty, and the water flowing from the hose made her want to pee so bad she thought she was going to wet her drawers. The thought occurred to her to go right then and there and spray herself with water and no one would know the difference. No one but her, that was. No, she had to find some place to go. But where? There was no outhouse that she could see, and she was desperate.

When Emma was sure no one was looking, she ran behind two cars on the railroad tracks. It was the only time in her life she'd wished she was a boy. How easy the whole business would have been. As quickly as she'd done anything in her life she dropped those overalls, praying all the time no one would sneak up on her. The puddle she was making in the dust grew from a river to a small lake. If ever she'd gotten a glimpse of how long eternity was, that was it. Getting caught with her pants down in broad daylight, squatting there over her own puddle of pee, would be worse than any hell she could imagine.

"Hey!" It was the boss's voice. Emma got those pants up and buckled quick. Even Houdini couldn't have done it faster. "Where's that kid who's supposed to be watering the elephants?" Boss Man yelled.

Emma grabbed her bucket and ran back between the cars.

A man no more than three feet tall pointed in her direction. "There!"

Already she had told three lies to get to see the circus and find the man in the photograph. She figured she'd try to even things out with one small truth. "Just had to pee . . . relieve myself is all, sir."

"Well, you get back and relieve them pachyderms, you hear?"

"Yes, sir. Right away, sir."

She couldn't remember which elephant she'd left off with, so she started back at number one. By the time she got to the ninth elephant for the third time, she felt as if she had drunk more water from that hose than the elephants had. By now those pachyderms thought the whole thing was great sport. Instead of drinking the water, they'd fill their trunks and squirt their backs. It was playtime, and Emma was the entertainment.

As she placed the filled bucket in front of pachyderm number three, he stuck his trunk into it like a straw drawing water. He lifted that trunk, and instead of drinking and instead of squirting his back, he let that water loose on Emma. She tried to leap out of the way, but pachyderm number two grabbed her hat with his trunk, and there she stood, wetter than a newborn kitten, with her curls exposed for all the world to see.

That's when the boss man with the cowboy hat walked up.

# CHAPTER SIX

## BOSS MAN

Hey there, Curly," the boss man said.

Quicker than a jackrabbit, Emma bent over, grabbed Granddad's damp, muddy fedora and shoved it back on her head.

Boss Man stood there grinning at her, as if he'd told a joke that could make a dead man laugh. But Emma knew. This joke was on her. She held her breath, waiting for him to tell her this was "no place for girls." Instead he said, "Looks like those elephants know who's boss."

She chuckled, from relief, mostly. "Yes, sir. Guess they do."

"And looks like you could use a trip to the barber's, too, kid," he said, pressing his hand on top of Granddad's fedora. "You don't want the world to be thinkin' you're a girl, now, do you?" Boss Man's eyes smiled along with his mouth.

"No, sir. Not me, sir."

"Well, do yourself a favor then and let your ma take her shears to that mane of yours. You don't want folks gettin' the idea you're somethin' you're not."

"No, sir." Holy cow. Was she ever stacking up the lies like pancakes on a Sunday!

Boss Man lifted his cowboy hat and rubbed the sweat off his brow, gawking at her with a puzzled expression. "You kinda remind me of someone. What's your name, kid?"

"Ah…Will," she said.

"Will what?"

"Reiner. Will Reiner."

*Lies. Lies. Lies.*

"Will, eh? Well, Will Reiner, mind if I call you Curly?"

"No, sir."

"Well now, Curly. See those bales of hay?"

"Yes, sir."

"Pull a couple close to the elephant line and break 'em open. And see that pitchfork over there? Take it and give each elephant about a quarter bale of hay. When you're through, come and see me."

"Yes, sir!" she said. Emma raced to the hay bales. Boss Man believed her lies, believed she was a boy! Then she recalled Boss Man's ready smile and odd expression and got a sinking feeling she might not be home free yet.

Pitching hay was easier than lugging buckets of water to nine thirsty elephants, but every time Emma opened a bale, she had to go back to the hose and get a drink. The heat and breathing in sawdust and hay made her mouth and throat scream for water. Once the hay was piled in front of the elephants, they settled down though. And except for the darn flies, those nine pachyderms might have been mistaken for statues. *Stomp, stomp, stomp* went the elephants' big feet trying to keep those flying devils from biting.

The morning was warming up and Emma's sweat was attracting its own company of hungry insects. With every breath came the smell of hay, dung, piss and her own sweat.

And the sounds! Elephants trumpeted, lions roared, and monkeys screeched. Everywhere there was hammering and the shouting of roustabouts. An exotic new world was making its home right here in Racine, Wisconsin, and she was part of it.

After Emma finished the hay job, she plopped down on a bale. Her stomach growled. While she munched on the apple she'd stuck in her pocket, she glanced around, hoping to catch a glimpse of some of the performers, hoping to spy Filippo the Flying Wonder. But no one wore costumes, so it was hard to tell who was who. Kids and grown-ups from town milled around the lot, gawking at the sights.

Roustabouts pounded the stakes into the ground where the Big Top would be. Groups of them clustered in circles around the stakes hammering and sweating as they pounded. Other men positioned poles on the ground around the tent.

"Hey!" Boss Man said. "Loafin' ain't gonna earn you a matinee ticket."

Emma jumped to attention. "No, sir!" She saluted like a soldier.

Boss Man looked at her like he was trying to hold back a smile. "King pole's about to go up. How 'bout lending the Big Top gang a hand?"

"You bet. Glad to!"

Boss Man blew a whistle, and workers who had been busy at other jobs hurried over to the Big Top's gigantic center pole lying on the ground.

"Go on," Boss Man said, motioning with his head toward the king pole and the fifty or so men who would raise it.

"Give 'em a hand, Curly."

"Yes, sir!" she sang. Emma ran to grab hold of a section of the king pole along with the gang of smelly, sweating men, pressing her palms and squeezing her fingers hard against the mighty solidity of the wood, wider than a telephone pole. All around her men chanted as they muscled that tent pole up.

Emma, too, pushed on the king pole with all her might, breathing deeply the smells of sweat and sour whiskey mixed with sawdust and hay. Goosebumps sprouted all over her as she listened to the men singing sea chanteys, feeling the surge of power as they pushed together to raise the pole.

When the center pole stood straight, high, and secure in the boxed-in hole that anchored it, she blurted, "We did it!"

The fellow next to her, a hairy, shirtless man, grinned and slapped her back. "Aye we did, Matey."

*Matey.* Music to her ears. She was one of them. How easy it was to fool people, so sinfully easy. In the next few minutes, with the help of horses, the other poles for the Big Top were hoisted into place. *Wham, bang, clang* the iron sledges sang as men pounded stakes into the earth.

"What are the stakes for?" she asked a roustabout.

"To secure the ropes and hold the canvas from blowing away," he said.

Emma sat on a hay bale and watched a crew of men unrolling bundles of canvas that had been placed around the lot. Another crew followed quickly along, lacing the sections of the Big Top together. Ropes from the canvas ran up over the tops of the poles and off to the circus horses, Emma

41

couldn't count how many, who stood at the ready.

Boss Man blew his whistle. At that signal, the horses moved forward and the huge canvas Big Top rose to the top of the king pole. Above her Emma could feel and hear the tent stretching up and out, welcoming in a cool breeze from the lake. All around the outside of the tent, men fastened the canvas to the stakes that had been pounded into the ground. Other men waited outside the tent by the ropes, ready to pull on them.

As she watched the Big Top quickly coming to life, out of the corner of her eye, Emma spotted a woman hurrying in her direction. She wore a wash dress like Mother's and a wide-brim hat that covered half her face. Emma ducked behind the hay bale. Could this woman be Mother? Had she gone to the Reiners' and found Emma wasn't there? Or had Clarence told her? What if she'd looked in her bureau and found the photograph missing? Emma felt her heart beating hard. She leaned against the bale, taking deep breaths.

*You're a bad person, Emma Monroe,* she thought. *You disobeyed your mother. Lied to her. You know what happens to bad people. They go to hell.*

Well, she guessed she probably was a bad person, but a girl needed to know who her father was. Didn't she? If Mother wasn't going to tell Emma who her father was, she had to find out for herself. Didn't she? Would God send her to hell for that?

Emma reached into her front pocket and pulled out the photograph. The handsome man stared back at her. She had to find him—and that was that.

She slipped the photograph back in the bib pocket and closed her eyes, imagining Filippo the Flying Wonder swinging high on a trapeze, flying across the Big Top. The scene cartwheeled across her imagination, while roustabouts chanted as they pulled the ropes to tighten the Big Top.

"Heave it, heavy down;

Hump back, jump back;

Take it back,

Break your back,

Hackenstack;

Down stake; next . . ."

After a few minutes, Emma peeked over the bale to see if the woman in the wash dress was still there. She didn't see her. She was safe . . . at least for now. But Emma gasped out loud at what she *did* see. In the short time she sat hidden behind the bale, a small city of tents had sprung up, more than a dozen.

A loud bell rang. "Chow time, Matey!" the hairy guy hollered.

The smell of bacon frying made Emma's mouth water.

"Curly!"

Emma turned to see Boss Man standing outside of the tent, motioning to her.

She ran over to him, hoping he'd tell her to go to the cook tent.

"Ready for the next job?"

"I'm kind of hungry, sir."

"Sorry, Curly. The cookhouse is only for bonafide circus folk. No rubes."

43

Emma's heart sank close to her growling, empty stomach. "Yes, sir." She hung her head and ground her heel into the dirt, hoping for a little mercy. When none came, she asked. "What's the next job?" Hungry or not, she had to keep working to earn that ticket.

"Putting up the stands and seats. It's a man's job, but maybe you can help haul the iron braces over to the stands after the roustabouts hook the stands together."

"You bet I can, sir." She tugged on the brim of Granddad's fedora.

Again, Boss Man smiled so big it put creases in his leathery face and he ogled her with that same puzzling expression.

"Then get goin', Curly. We ain't got all day. This here's a water stop. Matinee's at two. That's it. Then we push off."

"Yes, sir!" Emma shouted and ran to the pile of braces that Boss Man had pointed out.

She was just about to pick up the first brace when she heard a voice that made her heart leap into her throat.

"Emma!"

# CHAPTER SEVEN

## TROUBLE

Emma didn't have to turn around to know who was yelling her name. But she did anyway. Clarence and Teddy ran toward her all sweaty and red-faced.

"What in the heck are you doing?" Clarence asked.

She picked up an iron brace. "What does it look like I'm doing? Working. For a ticket to the Big Show. Like I told you."

"Honest?" Teddy said.

"You're going to be in a heap of trouble when your ma finds out," Clarence said. "And what are you doing in my overalls? And Granddad's hat?" Clarence bent over in mock laughter. "Boy, do you look dumb!"

"Let me try it on!" Teddy lunged at her, trying to snatch her hat. Emma blocked his hand with her arm.

That's when Boss Man walked up. "These your friends?"

"No!" She blurted, glad to tell the truth at last.

"What's your business here, boys? This ain't a play yard. We've got work to do."

Clarence, wearing a too-small pair of knickers and a dirty cap, puffed up his skinny self. "We can work," Clarence crowed.

Emma's heart stopped. She glared at her cousins, hard. Why should they weasel in on her plan? Already she'd put in hours of work. It wasn't fair.

"Well, guess I can't turn down an offer of more free labor," Boss Man said. "See that pile of seat planks? See those stands under the Big Top? You can give Curly here a hand. Carry them planks over to the stands there. No messing around, though. Or you're outta here. Got me?"

"Sure," her cousins said in one voice.

The roustabouts had already hooked the metal stands together under the Big Top. A huge pile of long, heavy seat planks that had to be put on the stands lay off to one side. After only about ten minutes of hauling those planks and setting them on the stands, her cousins started complaining.

"Man, it's hotter than the devil," Clarence said, sweat dripping off his face and onto the plank. Teddy carried the front end, Clarence the back, and Emma the middle. "And you," Clarence said, glaring at her. "You're not picking up any of this weight. Me and Teddy is doing all the work."

She let her hands go and stepped away from the plank.

Teddy turned his head around. "Hey! What's going on?"

"Nothing," Emma said, taking hold of the plank again. She grinned at Clarence and stuck out her tongue. She gave Teddy an ornery grin. They couldn't carry that plank without her. All those chin-ups and pull-ups on the monkey bars had made her strong.

On their way back from the stands to the plank pile, Boss Man yelled, "Hey, Curly, see if you can make your boys step it up a bit, to a man's pace, I mean." Again that grin.

"Why's he calling you Curly? Who is he, anyway?" Clarence whispered.

"The circus boss," Emma told him. "You'd better move it like he said, or we'll all be kicked out of here!"

The roustabouts, carrying the heavy planks on their shoulders, ignored them. They made the work look easy. Emma's back ached and the blisters on her hands stung. But she wasn't about to complain, not like her stupid cousins.

"Lift more weight, Emma," Teddy said. Now he was bringing up the rear, and Clarence was at the head. "You're not carrying your share!"

"What do you expect from a girl?" Clarence said.

"Shut up," she told them.

At that moment both Clarence and Teddy let go of the plank. For an instant, it was only Emma who held that plank in midair. And then she lay flat on her back, in the dust, with that plank on top of her chest. It hurt like heck, but she wasn't about to let on.

"All right. What's going on? I told you boys no messing around. I ain't got time for no shenanigans."

"It wasn't me, sir," Emma said, that plank still on top of her, tears smarting her eyes. "Those two dropped the plank!"

"Hmmm." This time Boss Man was trying *not* to grin. He stared at her lying there in the dust looking like Henny Penny holding up a piece of fallen sky. "Guess I can see that." He lifted the plank from her easy as if it was a popsicle stick and turned to her cousins. "OK, fellas. Curly was doin' fine before you came around. Vamoose. Off the circus grounds. Now."

"What? You're going to let *her* stay?" Clarence asked, pointing at Emma.

She stood up, dusting herself off.

"Her?" Boss Man said. "Who are you talking about?"

"Her," Clarence said. "She's a girl. Her name's Emma."

She could have killed him, right then and there in broad daylight with all those witnesses. Gladly. Instead, she looked straight into Boss Man's face and dared him to say she was a girl.

Boss Man stared back. She waited for those next words, the words that were going to determine her fate.

"Right," Boss Man said. "And I'm an Injun and my name is Pocahontas. Listen, if you two hooligans wanna earn a ticket into the Big Show, you're gonna have to do it on somebody else's time. Now vamoose!"

For once her cousins didn't talk back. Boss Man stood tall, over six feet. His bulging muscles glistened in the midday sun. Size, Emma guessed, they respected, because they turned tail and ran. Probably as glad as fleas on a pup they didn't have to work anymore, but madder than hornets that she got to stay, that Boss Man believed her and not them. At least her plan hadn't been ruined because of her meddling cousins.

Her cousins had gotten as far as the railroad spur when Clarence turned around. "You're gonna be in a heap of trouble if Aunt Saffy finds out you're here!" he yelled.

"Aunt?" Boss Man said. "Those boys your kin, Curly?"

Truth or lie?

She stared into Boss Man's coal-black eyes. He stared back.

"Yes. They're my cousins. We live together."

"Here…in Racine?

"Yes, sir."

48

"With your ma and pa?"

Emma felt her face get red. Why was Boss Man getting so nosey? She stared down at her boots and nodded.

"Your    pa,    what    does    he    do?"

"He's a milkman." Emma felt that familiar coiling in her stomach, the shame of not having a father, of having to lie. But lying about her father was her only choice, since she didn't know the truth.

"So, how's it you learned to work like a man and not them?"

Boss Man's words set her reeling. Why was Boss Man so goll darn sure she was a boy? That's what she wanted him to think, of course, but part of her wanted to let Boss Man know she was a girl—smart, and not afraid to work. But doing that would be crazy, it'd mean giving up everything she was working for.

"I guess they just don't want to see the circus as bad as I do."

"And why do you want to see the circus so bad, Curly?"

Emma shrugged and said, "Just do."

Boss Man laid a hand on her shoulder. "Probably got a bit of sawdust in your blood, Curly. Like me. There's no explainin' some things in this life. Like those freckles on your nose. Or hankerings that won't go away."

"Boss!" one of the roustabouts yelled, the hairy one that had called her Matey. "Someone from the city wants a word with you. Over yonder on the other side of the Big Top."

"Take a break, Curly. Then see if Sabu needs more help with the elephants," Boss Man said. He turned and strode off.

"Hey, kid," the roustabout said. "I think somebody's lookin' for you. Over there."

Emma turned to where he was pointing, and there stood Nan, waving with one hand and holding a lunch bucket with the other.

The roustabout gave Emma a friendly shove. "Looks like your girlfriend brought you lunch, Romeo."

# CHAPTER EIGHT

## NAN AND THE FREAK SHOW

You did it!" Nan giggled. "They think you're a boy. Did you get a ticket?"

"Not yet," Emma said. "Where's Lucky?"

"Home . . . with Mother," Nan said. "I hoped we could go to the Midway and I didn't think dogs were allowed." She stood on tip-toe, craning her neck to take in the sights. "Golly, it's a whole city here. So many tents! Have you seen Filippo the Flying Wonder yet?"

Emma shook her head. "The performers stay on the other side of the Big Top. No townies allowed there. Did she ask why you had him?"

"Who?"

"Lucky!"

"I told her you were helping at Dr. Rose's and he's allergic. Look! They're lining up for the parade." Nan pointed to the edge of the lot closest to 21st Street.

Emma turned her head. "Oh, my gosh. They are! I wish I could go watch!"

At the front of the line, rode the parade marshal mounted on a dapple-gray horse; two men on either side carried flags. Their horses flicked their heads and tugged at their reins. Behind them dancing girls stood on a carved and painted horse-drawn wagon, followed by a cage of monkeys hitched to four black horses.

"Look!" Nan squealed as six more dapple-grays pulling a wagon with polar bears joined the line. "Polar bears!"

"Oh my gosh. Those poor animals," Emma said. "How hot they must be in those fur coats! I can hardly stand it in these overalls and boots!"

Next, came Arabian ladies on horseback. Behind them paraded cages carrying lions, tigers, leopards, hyenas, sea lions, followed by camels and men in Turkish costumes astride zebras. Near the end of the line in front of the calliope, marched Emma's nine elephants wearing fancy halters and headdresses.

"Those are my elephants! The ones I watered!"

"Really?" Nan lifted her hat so she could see better. "Oh, Emma! I can't believe it. They're enormous!"

"Thirsty, too," Emma said as she watched her elephants lumber along, their trunks swinging, keeping time to the calliope's music. "After the parade, I'll probably get another watering job."

"And then you'll get your ticket?"

"I've got to!"

"But what if someone finds out you're a girl before then?"

Emma shuddered. She didn't want to think about that. The woman with the wide-brimmed hat flitted through her mind, and the funny way Boss Man looked at her sometimes.

"Make me leave, I guess. Do I really look like a boy? Be honest."

"Gee willakers, that's not a fair question, 'cause I know you. We've been friends since forever. But, here, let me take another look." Nan studied Emma, standing there all sweaty in Clarence's overalls and Granddad's fedora, then she grinned ear-to-ear. "Yeah, I swear you do. Smell like one, too. Though, you're much better looking than any silly Racine boy I know." Then Nan puckered up and pretended to smooch Emma. "So, what do you call yourself, Handsome?" she said, batting her eyelashes.

"Cut it out, Nan." Emma glanced around, sure she'd spy Boss Man or the roustabouts getting themselves an eye-full. But to her relief, everyone was too busy with their own affairs to be concerned with a couple townies.

"What *do* you call yourself?" Nan asked again.

"Will," Emma told Nan, giggling at the name she'd given herself.

"Look what I brought you . . .Will," she said, holding out a lunch bucket. "Lunch."

The mention of food made Emma forget everything except her empty stomach. "That was true blue of you, Nan. Whatcha got?"

"Peanut butter and jelly and lemonade. And a couple of your mama's cookies."

Emma would have rather it had been bologna with pickle and an orange Nehi but, of course, she didn't tell Nan that. Truth was, she was grateful Nan had thought of food when she hadn't. Besides, she could have eaten fried grasshoppers, she was so famished.

Nan and Emma found a spot of shade under one of the few trees near the edge of the circus grounds and plopped down to eat. While Nan nibbled at her sandwich, Emma devoured hers in a few fast bites and guzzled the lemonade. Music floated from the Midway while a fly flitted around Emma's mostly empty Mason jar.

Emma caught Nan staring at her. "You're so brave, Emma. I don't know any other girl who'd do what you're doing… except Nancy Drew maybe. And she's not even real." Nan said, her eyes filled with admiration.

"You could if you wanted something bad enough. You're lucky to have a father," Emma said. "And your mother positively dotes on you. Sometimes I wonder about my mother, if she cares about me at all."

"Of course she does, silly!"

"She never hugs me like your mother. She's so strict and…" Emma searched for the right word, "so…I don't know. Far away," she said at last, settling for a phrase that didn't really explain. "She's always so tired and crabby. I told her she should take Lydia Pinkham's compound like your mother does."

"She's not mean to you, though. Doesn't slap you, like Peggy Brown's mother does. Golly, I'd just die if Mama ever slapped me," Nan said, swatting the fly away from her lemonade.

"I don't know what I'd do if Mother ever slapped me," Emma said. "Run away with the circus maybe." She stared at the circus grounds, at all the people hurrying to get to the Midway, the music and sideshow barkers beckoning them, the aroma of hot dogs and roasted peanuts filling the hot, sticky air. Suddenly, Nan sat up and peered at Emma from under the brim of her hat. "What if you find out that this

Filippo guy *is* your father? What will you do?"

"I don't know. I haven't thought about that. I'll figure it out when it happens."

Nan smiled. "Of course, you will! Come on!" Nan grabbed Emma's hand and pulled her to her feet. "Let's look around!"

"I dunno, Nan. If Boss Man catches me loafing…"

"Oh, come on, just for a few minutes," Nan said, eyeing the Midway lined with the sideshows and concessions, the Big Top towering above everything, all flags flying.

"Let's take a peek at the freak shows," Nan said. She squeezed Emma's hand and her eyes got wide. "Maybe we'll see the boy with two heads!"

The question that sprung into Emma's mind was why the good Lord would give anybody two heads? Especially a boy, when most of the ones she'd seen, knew little enough what to do with one. But all the same, it was kind of thrilling to think of two heads coming out of the same body. Would one head talk to the other head? Would the other talk back? It kind of gave a person pause to think about the possibilities.

Emma glanced around to see if Boss Man was anywhere in sight. He wasn't. Maybe he was grabbing a bite to eat or off at the parade. What harm would it do to take a quick peek at the Midway? Besides, it was a chance to look for Filippo the Flying Wonder…unless he was off at the parade. Emma rubbed her hand over her front pocket that held the photograph, and strolled with Nan onto the Midway.

The sweet aroma of spun sugar drifted up her nose as they passed the first red and white concession stand lining one side of the Midway. Her mouth watered.

"Wish I'd brought some money," Nan said. "To buy us some cotton candy."

"Me, too," Emma said.

On the other side of the wide lane of straw and dust leading to the Big Top smaller tents stood, with wooden platforms out front. Banners and signs were plastered everywhere—HALF-MAN, HALF-WOMAN; TOM THUMB, SMALLEST MAN IN THE WORLD; THE GEEK, EATS LIVE CHICKENS; ATLAS, STRONGEST MAN IN THE WORLD, and LIVE CALF WITH TWO HEADS.

Just reading about all those exotic things made Emma quiver. This was just too exciting to be real—to think these strange and wonderful creatures were actually only yards, maybe feet, from her! But not a one of those wonders was about at that moment. And she didn't have the dime for admission. She imagined them inside their tents…doing what? It boggled the imagination and gave her goose bumps.

Feeling scared, excited, and giddy all at the same time, Emma and Nan ambled closer to the first tent of the side show—TINA, FATTEST WOMAN IN THE WORLD.

There, to Emma's surprise, on the outside platform near the ticket stand, sat Tina herself in a huge rocking chair. She was dressed in a skimpy romper, sunning and fanning her face with a piece of cardboard. Emma had never seen so much skin on any one person in her life, yards and yards of it, all pink and glistening with perspiration. Holy cow! How does a person grow so much fat and the skin to cover it? The body is certainly one remarkable invention.

The Fat Lady smiled at them, and as she did, her eyes disappeared under rolls of cheek fat. "How you doin', Sonny?" the Fat Lady said to Emma.

Nan nudged Emma, then started giggling, which made Emma laugh, too, even though she didn't want to. Not at all. But something was tickling her like the devil on the inside. And the more she didn't want to laugh, the more she did. The more she thought about how they must be hurting poor Tina's feelings, the more she couldn't stop laughing. Then, as if caught in the grip of their giggles, the Fat Lady started laughing too. Her blubber shook and shimmied like Jell-O. Tina laughed so hard Emma worried she'd rock herself right out of that chair. What would she and Nan do if Tina catapulted herself right out of that chair and landed on them? Holy cow!

It seemed Tina would never stop laughing and rocking, so Emma grabbed Nan's hand and pulled her farther down the Midway.

"Look," Nan said, pointing to a sign that said, THE GEEK WHO EATS LIVE CHICKENS.

Emma wondered what sort of reception they might get from the Geek if he were sitting outside his tent. Emma pictured the Geek as a small man with a very large head, beady red eyes, and a huge mouth frothing with saliva and chicken feathers.

"Let's go see the animals," Emma said. "We can see them for free. The freak shows seem kind of...freaky."

Emma and Nan ran toward the menagerie tent that

displayed the animals. When they stepped inside, they could smell the musky scent of a barnyard, even though the cages that hadn't been used in the parade sat empty.

"Look!" Nan said, pointing to the opposite end of the menagerie where a section of the tent had been lifted, exposing the view on the other side. "A lion tamer!"

Just outside the menagerie tent stood a metal cage with a man inside cracking a whip. Emma and Nan ran through the menagerie to get a closer look.

A sign across the cage read: CAT MAN TAMES SIMBA THE LION. Inside, Cat Man was shouting and snapping his whip, trying to get a lion to jump through a hoop onto a platform. Fat Simba just lay there making a great roaring yawn as if plain bored.

Cat Man's whip snapped, and swear words flew from his mouth. His face dripped with sweat, but Simba didn't move a muscle. "You worthless animal!" Cat Man shouted.

Simba yawned.

Nan giggled, but Cat Man's shouting and the sound of the cracking whip sent a cold chill down Emma's spine. What a way to treat an animal!

"Hey kid, *heiraus!*" someone shouted.

It was Sabu, the Elephant Man, back from the parade carrying a long pole with a sharp silver point and hook. Except for a pair of baggy shorts and one of those cloth hats Indian swamis wear, he was naked and his skin painted with yellow grease paint.

"*Heiraus,*" Nan whispered. "That's a German swear word. I've heard my grandfather say it. It means get the heck of out of here."

So, Sabu was a fake, Emma thought, not from India at all. But grease paint or not, he sure did know his elephants.

He stood directly in front of them now, so close that Emma could see yellow paint caked in the creases on his chest. "Hey," Sabu said, his voice softening. "You're the kid what watered my sweethearts, *nicht*, ain't you?" Sabu said.

Emma nodded.

"*Gutt*, well go do it again. That's a good boy."

Nan put her hand to her mouth to hide her giggling, staring at the half-naked Sabu.

"Guess I'd better go," Nan whispered.

At that moment parading llamas, horses, ponies and brightly painted animal cages housing wild cargo began pouring into the back entrance of the menagerie tent. Nan's hand flew to her mouth. "Oh my gosh! The animals are back! Let's look!"

"I need to get back to work, Nan," Emma said, disappointed she couldn't stay to get a closer look at the gorillas, the bears, and the monkeys.

Emma and Nan made their way through the menagerie, side-stepping folks gawking at the animals as they tried to get into the tent from the Midway entrance.

"I wonder what time it is?" Emma said as they stepped out onto the now crowded Midway.

"About noon, I think," Nan said.

"Good. That means Mother won't be looking for me. Not yet, anyway…not unless Clarence squealed on me. I saw a woman who looked like her this morning and thought I was done for."

"What if she finds out you're here? Aren't you scared stiff she'll skin you alive?"

"Sure I am. But I can't quit now." Emma picked up her pace. "I'm going to see the circus and find my father come hell or high water."

Nan gasped at Emma's brazenness, swearing like a sailor. But Emma liked the feeling it gave her, as if saying those words gave her the power to make them happen.

"I hope you do get a ticket," Nan said as they passed the ticket wagon. "And I hope you find your father. I truly do!" Nan ran off down the Midway, the empty lunch bucket bouncing against her leg.

"Thanks for coming and bringing lunch!" Emma called as she watched Nan hurry off the circus lot. "Give Lucky a hug for me! See you at the Fourth of July party!"

Emma ran back to the elephants, back to the buckets, the hose, and the water. She knew they'd be awfully thirsty after their long walk in the heat. And she was right. They slurped up enough water to empty Lake Michigan.

In less than half an hour, she was done watering the elephants. Time to search for Boss Man. Darn if she didn't comb the whole Midway area for another half hour and not see him anywhere. He had to show up pretty soon. The matinee was about to begin and she needed that ticket. She needed to get inside the Big Top before Mother found her.

Dozens of people stood in a long line at the ticket wagon. Everyone and everything looked ready to go.

So where was Boss Man? Maybe he'd finished his job for

the day. What if he'd left the circus grounds and right now was sitting in one of those speakeasies on State Street?

"You still here, Curly?"

Boss Man's deep voice made her nearly jump out of her skin. She spun around.

He stood behind her, smelling of cologne and sporting a crisp white shirt—that made his face look even tanner—black trousers, brown cowboy boots, and the cowboy hat, which he tipped at her. Why?

She cleared her throat to speak, trying to make her voice come out low. "I just finished another job for Sabu, watering the elephants. I was hoping you'd give me a ticket now for the matinee."

"You did, did you? Well, now…why don't you just sneak under the tent like the rest of the lot lice?"

*Lot lice!* Boss Man's words took her breath away. "Because…because I want a proper seat, that's why!" Emma could feel her stomach burning as if she'd swallowed the fire-eater's torch. "I want to see everything…feel a part of it, like I belong, not like some nose-picking…rube!"

Boss Man laughed and that made her face burn even more.

"I've worked hard! Ask Sabu. I've earned that ticket!" Emma cried, her voice breaking.

Boss Man smiled. Then he opened up his wallet that hung by a chain on his belt. "You're right, kid, you've earned it," Boss Man said, handing her a general admission ticket. "But you can take off that hat now…missy."

# CHAPTER NINE

## UNDER THE BIG TOP

You know I'm not a boy?" Emma asked, horrified.

"Since the minute I laid eyes on you."

"But you let me work."

"I don't have nothin' against girls. Hell, you're as good a worker as any boy, nearly as strong, smarter, and . . ." Boss Man smiled. "A mite better looking, I'd add. You remind me of a girl I once knew."

Emma felt herself blushing.

"Enjoy the circus, missy. But better run along, if you want to get a good seat."

She didn't know what to say or hardly even what to do. All she knew was that her face felt flushed, as warm as if she'd been standing in front of a crackling fire, and inside her, near her heart, she felt full of the strangest feelings, feelings so new they didn't seem to belong to her. And then she heard Nan's voice.

"Will! Yoo-hoo! Over here!"

Startled, she looked across the circus lot at Nan who stood under the tree where they'd had lunch, waving frantically. What was Nan doing here again? And why did she look so desperate?

Then, remembering her manners, she turned back to Boss Man. "Thank you for the ticket, thank you very much!"

Boss Man tipped his hat and off Emma flew toward Nan.

"Is something wrong?" Emma asked, taking deep breaths. "Why are you back?"

"Clarence and Teddy. They said your mother was looking for you!"

"Oh, my gosh! I've got to get inside the Big Top before Mother finds me!"

"You got a ticket?"

Emma held out the precious yellow ticket with the black letters. *Admit One. Hackenstack's Most Spectacular Show on Earth.*

Nan grinned. "Oh, Emma!"

"Wish me luck," Emma said, running toward the Midway. Soon she would see him, Filippo the Flying Wonder! The man who very possibly was her very own father.

But first she had to get inside the Big Top before Mother found *her.*

∞

The Midway swarmed with people. A long line had formed at the ticket wagon and a longer line snaked toward the Big Top entrance.

Emma pulled Granddad's fedora low on her forehead, keeping her eyes glued to the ground as she weaved her way through the crowd, dodging kids carrying balloons, toy monkeys on a stick, and cotton candy. She didn't want to see anyone she knew. Even in overalls and a fedora someone might recognize her. The thought of Mother finding her before she was safe inside the Big Top made her stomach knot up.

"Step right up, Ladies and Gentlemen," a sideshow barker

called. "Get your tickets to cast your eyes upon exotic, never-seen-before wonders that will thrill and amaze. And what you see on the banners outside, you'll witness in living reality on the inside. Step right up!"

Emma glanced up at the banner showing Fat Lady Tina and wondered how Tina felt about people gawking at her in her satin rompers, her ample flesh exposed for all the world to see. Tina seemed like a nice person, someone who you could have fun joking around with. She certainly knew how to laugh!

"Hot dogs! Popcorn! Cotton candy!" concessionaires shouted. The smell of hot dogs, roasted peanuts, and popcorn made Emma's mouth water but, of course, she had no money for any of it.

The band started playing and people began making their way to the Big Top. The show was going to begin soon.

Hurrying to take her place at the end of the crowded line, Emma looked around for Mother. When she didn't see her, Emma gave a silent prayer of thanks.

The kid in front of her pinched his nose shut. "Somebody has BO," he said.

"Woodrow!" a tall lady next to him said. "Don't be rude."

The kid, of course, meant her. Who else could it have been? Spending the morning watering elephants, hoisting the Big Top, and carrying planks for the bleachers made her smell as ripe as Granddad's Limburger cheese. Not the odor she wanted, since she was soon going to meet the handsome Filippo the Flying Wonder. Holy cow, he'd take one whiff of her and run the other way! This matter of personal hygiene posed a problem she hadn't considered until this moment. When and how could she find a way to wash?

When the line started to move, Emma's heart began to beat faster. She reached inside her pants pocket, felt for the ticket, and held it tight.

"Ticket," the man said when Emma finally reached the podium where the ticket taker sat. He had dark bushy eyebrows, blood-shot eyes, and a mustache that fell over his lip.

"Ticket!" the man repeated. "Got a ticket or not, Huck?"

Emma handed him her ticket. "Could I have a stub…for a souvenir?"

The man scowled, but tore the ticket, handing Emma half. She stuck the stub in her front pocket next to the photograph.

As she stepped inside the Big Top, Emma's heart nearly jumped into her throat. How amazing it looked! Dozens of poles holding up the enormous canvas roof jutted every which way, wires criss-crossed, lights beamed, ropes dangled. Ripples of excitement skittered through her as she stared at the trapezes suspended high above the sawdust floor.

"Over there, Sonny," the usher said, pointing to an empty spot in the third row. Emma hurried to grab the seat while the band played and the trombones *oom-pah-pahed*.

"Popcorn, fresh roasted peanuts! Get 'em while they're hot! Ice cold lemonade!" candy butchers shouted. Her throat felt dry as sawdust. If only she had a nickel.

In front of her, down on the track, a clown dressed in an oversized policeman's uniform and huge floppy shoes twirled a baton and pretended to whack a girl in the front row, but whopped himself on the head instead. The girl shrieked and Emma giggled. Tiny bubbles tickled her insides. And then tears suddenly stung at her eyes. How silly! Laughing and crying at the same time! Like sweet and salty mixed together. Soon she would see the man who might be her father.

Emma gazed around the Big Top. She wanted to remember everything, press it on her brain so she wouldn't forget a thing—the sights, smells, and sounds. But before she had a chance, the lights dimmed, a drum rolled, and the band began playing a tune that made her feet want to dance. When the lights brightened again, Emma perched on the edge of her seat. Down on the hippodrome track paraded jugglers and acrobats, clowns on foot and in wagons, and carved and painted cages carrying exotic animals. There were horses with bareback riders, camels, and *her* elephants—a dazzling cavalcade of glitter, spangle, and music.

Before the last elephant had marched from the tent, the ringmaster shouted, "Ladies and Gentleman, children of all ages, now direct your attention to ring number three where the amazing Wonder Bears will perform feats of unparalleled skill and dazzling grace!"

In ring number three, six brown bears wearing yellow ballet skirts danced around on their hind legs like giant teddy bear ballerinas. They stood on their forepaws, their hind legs in the air. They laid on their backs twirling barrels with their hind feet. They caught balls thrown by their trainers. They looked like they were having fun. Emma hoped they were.

The crowd went wild over their antics, clapping and cheering. It was hard to believe these were honest-to-goodness bears and not people wearing bear costumes. Who could imagine bears riding bicycles, juggling, skating, and dancing? Oh, if only Nan were here to see it all.

"Ladies and Gentleman, now in the center ring—Dominic the Daring and his prides of the jungle."

Emma focused her eyes on the center ring. A dozen or more striped tigers swaggered inside a large cage in the center ring. Their fierce roars sent chills up and down her spine. Dominic the Daring carried a baton, not a whip like Cat Man with bored Simba. When Dominic waved his baton, he looked like a bandleader—*la, la, la, la!* And, holy cow, if that waving baton didn't get those tigers quietly gathered together, sitting like a bunch of pussycats in a sunny window! Then Dominic picked up a hoop. In the next instant, the hoop was filled with dancing flames and, one after the other, the tigers leaped through the fiery hoop.

"Ohhhh!" the crowd roared.

"Lord have mercy!" a woman behind her said. "Those poor, beautiful animals!"

"It's just an act, Gladys," a man said. "They're fine."

Emma hoped he was right. The animal acts were thrilling and a wonder to behold, still how did the animals feel about all this? She hoped they thought it was all great fun.

For the next several acts, there was something going on in all three rings at once. Emma's gaze jumped from one ring to another. She didn't want to miss a thing.

Then she saw Sabu leading the elephants she had hayed and watered that morning into the Big Top. It was their turn!

Emma grinned with pride watching those mammoth

pachyderms dance as gracefully as any human dancer one one-hundredth their size. Emma whistled and clapped and cheered for her elephants.

When the elephants paraded off with Sabu, the ringmaster announced, "And now, Ladies and Gentlemen, the moment you have been waiting for—the one, the only, the death-defying Flying Santinis—Gabriele, Filippo, and Maria!"

Emma craned her neck toward the performers' entrance to get her first look at him—Filippo the Flying Wonder. And there he was, she was sure of it, the man on the right side of Maria. Butterflies fluttered in her stomach. She clapped loudly as the three Flying Santinis pranced into the center ring with long, flowing capes draped over their shoulders. They smiled, their arms wide, reaching out to greet the audience, turning in every direction while the band played and the people clapped and cheered. Emma leaned forward in her seat, staring hard at the man to Maria's right, the man the ringmaster had called Filippo. If only he would turn and look at her. She needed so desperately to see his face. Was his the same face as the one in the photograph?

Emma laid her hand on the bib pocket where the photograph lay against her heart and held her breath.

*Walk over here. Walk closer.* Emma prayed. *Walk closer!*

# CHAPTER TEN

## FILIPPO THE FLYING WONDER

But Emma's silent prayer was not answered. Instead of walking closer to where she sat, Filippo, Gabriele, and Maria turned to the other side of the tent, swirled off their capes and handed them to a man who stood at the edge of the ring.

Gabriele kicked off a pair of white clogs, grabbed the edge of the net, and flipped over onto it. Then, he climbed a rope that led to a trapeze hanging high above the center ring. At the same time, Filippo and Maria climbed a rope ladder to a platform opposite Gabriele. Then Maria unhooked a trapeze and pushed it high. Standing in the center of the platform, Maria grabbed the bar as it flew back to her, swung out on it, turned around, and returned to the platform smiling, standing tall, arms outspread. Filippo did the same, only his swing was higher and his return to the platform showier.

As the band began a waltz tune, Maria swung out on the trapeze, did a twisting somersault, then let go in midair. Emma gasped. A split second later, Gabriele, hanging upside down on the other trapeze, caught Maria. Cymbals clashed and the audience exploded into applause. Gabriele and Maria swayed together, Maria hanging from his grasp, Gabriele dangling upside down on the bar, until Maria caught the empty flying trapeze and returned to the platform.

Next was Filippo's turn. Emma wiped her sweaty hands

69

on her overalls and craned her neck to watch the man who just might be her very own father.

Drums rolled. Filippo grabbed onto the trapeze, then swung higher and higher, so high Emma felt dizzy. Her palms sweat even more, her feet too. She held her breath when she heard Maria shout, "Break!" Filippo, his body straight as a board, his toes nearly touching the top of the tent, let go of the bar and for a split second floated in mid-air. The audience gasped and Gabriele grabbed Filippo by the wrists. Emma let out the breath she had been holding and clapped her blistery hands.

While the band played, Filippo, Gabriele, and Maria soared high above the net and the sawdust, twisting and spinning. When they flew, letting go of the trapeze, they looked like birds in the air, swooping from branch to branch as if gravity had no hold on them at all. It was danger and glory all at once. The crowd gasped whenever Maria or Filippo let go and somersaulted or pirouetted in mid-air, falling, falling until finally they reached Gabriele who hung upside down with his knees clamped tight around the bar.

Emma's palms felt cold and wet and her stomach quivered. But, oh, more than anything, she wanted to soar like the Santinis, to feel the thrill and freedom of flying!

Then an idea came to her so quickly and with such clarity, it startled her. What if Filippo could teach her? Teach her to fly through the air like he did? The idea was thrilling and terrifying—all at once—and she wondered why she hadn't thought of it before. Maybe Boss Man was right—maybe the circus was in her blood, really and truly part of who she was.

"And now, ladies and gentleman," the ringmaster announced. "You are about to witness the most amazing, death-defying trick in circus history. Please, direct your attention to Filippo the Flying Wonder as he prepares to attempt the TRIPLE somersault!"

Murmurs trickled through the audience.

"Silence, please!" the ringmaster called.

A hush fell over the audience. The woman next to Emma bent close to her and whispered, "A triple somersault, like the great Codona. He could break his neck...if he fell."

"I can't watch," the woman behind Emma moaned.

Emma's stomach lurched. She wanted to cover her eyes, but she couldn't. She lifted her head toward the top of the tent, eyes riveted on the platform a hundred feet above the floor where Filippo stood. There was a net . . . if he did fall . . . but still . . .

Filippo grabbed the trapeze bar and yelled "Listo!"

Drums rolled softly as Gabriele, swinging on the trapeze, flipped himself upside down and wrapped his legs around the ropes that held the bar. "Hep!" he called. The eerie word echoed through the tent, while the soft drum roll increased its tempo.

Filippo, trapeze bar in hand, leaped from the platform and swung. Higher and higher he soared until Emma thought he would hit the roof of the Big Top. The drums rolled louder and Emma's heart thudded at its own frantic pace. She covered her ears, but not her eyes. At the height of the arc, Filippo swung so high his head touched the top of the tent.

"Break!" Maria shouted.

Filippo hurled his body heavenward, let go of the trapeze and spun, somersaulting backwards like a whirling ball.

The crowd gasped.

Emma's heart leaped into her throat.

Where was the catcher?

Cymbals clashed.

A split second later, a smiling Filippo dangled from Gabriele's grasp.

A loud cymbal crashed—*triumph*!

The crowd let out one huge sigh as Filippo pirouetted back to the bar and mounted the pedestal. *Tah dah*! boomed the band, then started a rousing tune while the audience broke into applause like thunder.

Emma stomped her feet and clapped her hands until her palms stung. Tears rolled out of the corners of her eyes as Filippo climbed down a rope to the center ring and bowed as if to say, "I am the greatest"—and he was.

After his first bow, Filippo stood up and walked closer to her section of the tent to take another bow. When he stood up from his bow and looked up at the audience what she saw took her breath away. He *did* look like the man in the photograph. Was this amazing man who now stood only yards in front of her truly her very own father?

# Chapter Eleven

## No Townies Allowed!

The crowd was still applauding when Filippo, Gabriele, and Maria pranced toward the performer's entrance, waving, smiling and blowing kisses. Emma caught one of Filippo's kisses and blew back her own.

At that moment, she knew what she had to do. Now was her chance. Maybe her only chance.

"Excuse me," she repeated as she made her way down the crowded row toward the aisle, bumping into knees, stepping on toes. She had to get to the performers' entrance that led to the circus backyard. She had to find Filippo before he disappeared forever.

"Hey! Down in front!" people yelled.

Just as she stepped onto the sawdust floor of the hippodrome track, clowns sprang through the performers' entrance. Quickly she side-stepped the barrage of clowns in her desperate attempt to get out of the tent and find Filippo. But instead of reaching the outside, she found herself swept along in a frenzy of flapping feet, honking noses, and tooting horns. One clown snatched her hat, her hair tumbling out. He pulled off his cone-shaped hat and plunked Granddad's fedora on his bald head. Then he jammed his own pointy hat on her head, snapped the rubber band under her chin, and clapped his white-gloved hands, his painted smile a mile wide.

"Just go along with this, kid," the clown whispered. "It'll be fun." Two other clowns scooped her up by the elbows and carried her along with them. The crowd howled.

When they reached the center ring, the clowns tossed Emma into a blanket and began flinging her in the air. Up she flew and down she fell while the band played and the crowd hooted. Emma's stomach tickled, but the clown was wrong. She wasn't having fun. The clowns had spoiled her chance to find Filippo. But that wasn't the worst of it. What if Mother stood watching inside the Big Top?

As if reading her thoughts, the clowns cocooned the scratchy, mildew and hay-smelling blanket around her. Her stomach squeezed up the nearly digested peanut butter and lemonade. She swallowed the bitterness back down . . . but barely. She felt herself being carried, bounced and jounced, while the band played and the audience roared.

After what seemed like an eternity, the sack opened and she toppled onto the dusty ground outside the tent. Dark clouds had gathered in the sky, throwing the circus lot under their shadows. The clown wearing Granddad's fedora bent over and yanked his own hat off Emma. He stared at her hair. "Here's your hat, girlie. You did great," he said, handing her Granddad's fedora and a red-checkered handkerchief. "A little souvenir for you."

"Thank you," Emma said, stuffing the handkerchief in her pants pocket.

"Now back inside with you. No townies in the backyard."

Emma smiled at the clown, but didn't get up. She hoped he would disappear into the tent where she had seen the other clowns go. But he just stood there as if waiting to make sure she wasn't going to wander the backyard where she didn't belong.

Horses and bareback riders began lining up at the performers' entrance. Music spilled from the Big Top and the horses started high-stepping and bobbing their plumed heads. Their lady riders' costumes glittered with a million sequins, as the horses pranced through the performers' entrance.

"Go, kid!" the clown said. "You don't want to miss the Liberty Show."

"No, sir." Emma jumped up and dusted the sawdust off her behind. Quickly, she scurried around the last horse in line, putting the spotted pony between herself and the clown. Then she ducked behind the canvas flap at the tent's backdoor. While she waited for the clown to leave, Emma surveyed the backyard. Little kids chased each other, running in between the many tents and wagons. Clothes hung on lines draped from tent ropes. Several acrobats practiced their routines. And then Emma spotted the menagerie cages, now empty, being rolled toward the railroad flatcars that waited on the track. Workers, many of them black men, pulled down the menagerie and sideshow tents while inside the Big Top the show went on. The circus was coming down and the matinee hadn't even ended yet! How long before the whole circus would be gone? She had to find Filippo before she was caught or kicked out.

That's when she spotted the watering trough. A bucket stood beside it, like a pot of gold at the end of a rainbow.

Of course! She would pretend to be the water boy here in the backyard just as she had been for Boss Man and Sabu that morning. She would fill the bucket and provide water for any thirsty animal she saw. And then she would wash herself.

Music for the equestrian act still echoed from the Big Top. At the far end of the backyard, she spotted her elephants now wearing bright red harnesses on their gigantic heads. They lumbered toward the performers' entrance with Sabu leading them, dressed in his fake swami suit. Ladies in fancy ruffled costumes—with long, white satin gloves and feathered headdresses—perched atop the mammoth beasts.

Sabu spotted Emma with her bucket. "You still here! *Nicht!* Away!" He flicked a hand at her. "No water. No pissing elephants!" Sabu yelled. "Stupid boy."

Not knowing what else to do, Emma tipped the bucket, dumping the water, and ran past Sabu and the line of elephants—to where, she had no idea. She spotted a circus wagon at the far end of the lot, thinking she could duck behind it and not be seen. With her eyes fixed on the wagon, she stepped in a soft pile of elephant dung.

"Hey, Sonny. What you doing in the backyard?" a voice asked. It was Tina, waddling between two tents. She had changed from her rompers into a regular woman's dress.

"Um . . . I need to see Filippo," Emma said.

"The Flying Wonder?"

Emma nodded.

Tina started laughing so hard her whole body shook. This lady sure did find things amusing. "That dressing tent down there . . . next to Clown Alley," Tina said when she had stopped laughing. "Hey, what's your business with him?"

Emma thought fast. "Ah . . . got an important message for him."

"Important message, eh?" Tina said. "What's your name, kid? You're a townie, aren't you?" She stared at Emma, her eyes like shiny bits of coal stuck into the plump cheeks of a snowman. Tina placed her warm hand on Emma's shoulder. "I wouldn't bother Mr. Filippo now if I were you." She winked and wobbled toward the waiting train cars.

Of course she would bother Filippo. She hadn't come this far to worry about manners. She found the hose she'd used earlier that day and rinsed out the bucket. She had to try to make herself presentable. Her entire body felt sticky with sweat. Even though the clouds blocked the worst of the sun's heat, the air was a blanket. The smells—animal and human—made her stomach churn.

She wiped the foul-smelling elephant dung off her boots on a hay bale. With the water from the hose, she rinsed the checkered handkerchief the clown had given her and ran back behind the empty circus wagon. Here she washed her face, underarms, and hands with the handkerchief. When she thought she'd done as good a job as she could, she wiped the rest of the dung off her boots. By now that handkerchief was brown with filth, her own and the elephants'. Her hair was another matter. That would have to stay tucked in the fedora. She couldn't risk being caught and thrown out now.

A chill skittered down her spine.

What would Filippo be like? And what would he think of *her*?

Emma rinsed out the handkerchief as best she could and walked toward the tent Tina had said was Filippo's.

She heard voices—a man's…and then a woman's.

The woman giggled.

The sounds from inside the tent made Emma blush. They were probably kissing. Had Tina been wrong about this being Filippo's tent? Was the man's voice she heard not Filippo's?

Strangely, Emma felt relieved that the man inside the tent may not be Filippo. So, who, then, was inside the tent? And where was Filippo?

"Curly!" Boss Man's voice behind her nearly startled her out of her underwear. "What are you doing here? Why aren't you at the matinee?" he asked. This time he wasn't smiling.

Her heart thumped like a tom-tom, as Boss Man stood staring at her, waiting for her answer. What would she say, do? Maybe it was time for the truth.

Emma pulled the photograph from her bib pocket and handed it to Boss Man. She watched his face, waiting for him to say something.

"Where'd you get this?" Boss Man asked.

She tried to read his eyes, those eyes that were now studying her. "It belongs to my . . . my mother," Emma said.

"Oh…my…God," he said and shook his head. "I thought maybe. Jesus, Mary, and Joseph. Hold on, Curly." He opened the flap of the tent and called inside. "Romeo, you have a visitor."

"Not now!" the man said.

"This is someone I think you ought to meet," Boss Man said.

Emma held her breath, wondering if the man would come out. Wondering *who* would come out. The air was thick and still, the mid-afternoon dark as twilight. Thunder rumbled in the distance. Finally, the canvas flap on the tent opened and there he stood, just a few feet from her—Filippo the Flying Wonder, half naked, his bare chest shiny with sweat, his dark hair as badly in need of a comb as hers, a cigarette dangling from his lips. When Emma finally took a breath, it was of sweat and tobacco.

"Sapphira's daughter," Boss Man told Filippo, then handed him the photograph.

Filippo's sleepy eyes became wide awake. "*Mio Dio!*" he said.

Emma bit her lip to keep from crying. She stared at Filippo. Close up he didn't look quite like she thought he would, like the man who took her breath away only a few minutes earlier under the Big Top.

Before she could say anything, Emma heard barking. She turned and there was Lucky racing toward her. He jumped up on her and tried to lick her face.

Emma fell to her knees and wrapped her arms around Lucky. "Oh, buddy," she whispered. "You're not supposed to be here."

"Emma!" someone shouted.

When Emma turned in the direction of the shout, there stood Clarence and Teddy at the fence that circled the back lot. "Your ma's coming!" Teddy yelled.

Emma's heart nearly stopped and then started thudding hard. Before she could consider what Mother would do if she found her here at the circus, a bare-footed woman wearing a pink satin robe appeared at the tent door. "Popo, what's going on? You've got to get dressed. The finale's in five minutes."

The man—Filippo, Popo, Romeo, whoever he was—started toward the tent door, then turned to Emma. "Meet me here after the matinee," he told her, his voice no longer gruff. He smiled and scratched his head. "Sapphira's baby girl. Now ain't that something?"

Just as Filippo disappeared inside the tent, thunder boomed and the sky opened up. Pea-size hail pelleted tents and yard. Lucky barked frantically.

"Get him out of here!" Boss Man said. "Go." He pointed at a gate at the far end of the backyard not too far from where Clarence and Teddy had stood a few minutes earlier.

Emma ran, Lucky beside her, toward the gate and the empty railroad car where she told Nan she would be if she had to hide. Now she did have to hide, from the pouring rain and from the awful feeling that maybe she had done something terribly wrong in disobeying Mother, coming to the circus to try and find her father. Still, she didn't know for certain that this man, Filippo, the Flying Wonder, *was* her father. But one thing she did know. She couldn't leave the circus grounds until she found out.

# Chapter Twelve

## Caught

By the time Emma reached the boxcar, Granddad's fedora and Clarence's overalls had soaked up half the sky. She climbed the ladder, Lucky close behind her, and crashed through the open doors, tripping and falling flat on her face.

Inside sat Clarence and Teddy, resting on a bale of hay, laughing at her.

"Shut up, you stinking tattletales," she yelled. "Why'd you tell Mother where I was?"

"Aunt Sapphira made us tell," Teddy said.

"You were supposed to help at Dr. Rose's. Remember?" Clarence said, all high-hat. "But, no, you were off at the circus, exactly where your ma told you not to go. When you gonna grow up, Emma? Did you really think you'd get away with this?"

"Aunt Saffy came home to get you," Teddy said. "Then Lucky came. We're no tattletales. She had to whoop it out of us." He grinned.

Emma glared at her cousins, hands on hips. "Mother would never whoop you. Though she should in my opinion."

"Don't get so hoity-toity, Emma Monroe," Clarence said. "We came here to warn you about your ma. Remember?"

"Yeah," Teddy said, resting his elbows on his knees, chin in his hands. "Did you get to see the circus? Was it keen?"

Emma nodded. "Most spectacular show on earth." She shivered, from the wet clothes or remembering Filippo's triple somersault, she couldn't tell.

"So," Clarence said. "Why aren't you at the matinee anyhow? What were you doing with Boss Man and that other fellow?"

"None of your beeswax," she said, rubbing her hands over her arms, trying to get warm. Lucky made himself comfortable on the dirty boxcar floor.

"Come on, Emma," Clarence said. "What are you up to now, besides a heap of trouble?"

"You wouldn't believe me if I did tell you . . . which I'm not." Hers was a juicy plum of a secret, one that was hard not to crow like a barnyard cock about—the possibility of having a father who was a famous circus performer.

"Tell us, Emma. Please?" Teddy pleaded.

Emma stared at her cousins, itching to tell. "That man with Boss Man? That was Filippo the Flying Wonder. And, I think he's my father!"

"What?" Clarence said. "You're looney!"

Teddy laughed. "You ain't got a pa."

"Yeah," Clarence said. "You're a bastard."

Emma lunged at Clarence and pounded him with her fists. Lucky stood up and barked. "You take that back!" Emma shouted. Tears stung at the corners of her eyes.

"Can't take back the truth, Emma. Your ma was never married to your pa. That makes you illegitimate, a bastard, no matter how you look at it."

Emma unclenched her fists. She could hear her heart

pounding. "You don't know that!"

"I heard my ma tell Pa."

"That doesn't make it the truth!"

"So, why doesn't your ma ever talk about your pa?"

"Doesn't matter," Emma said. Which was a lie. It mattered very much.

Why had she shared her precious secret with her stupid cousins anyway? And she had almost showed them the photograph. The photograph! Where was it? She had given it to Boss Man outside of Filippo's tent. Then what? She couldn't remember. She had to get it back!

"So, what are you planning to do now? Run away with the circus?" Clarence teased. "You go home, your ma's probably gonna lock you up forever."

"But whoop you first," Teddy said. "When she finds you. You *should* run away and join the circus."

"Maybe I will." She glowered at her cousins, a couple of stupid, lying farm boys with no father of their own to speak of, since he was in faraway California somewhere. "Maybe I will join the circus."

"Do it," Teddy said. "You should. *I* would."

"She won't," Clarence said. "Emma's just fooling with us."

"You'll be eating your words soon enough. I'm meeting Filippo the Flying Wonder after the matinee. I'll convince him to let me come with the circus, teach me to fly—a father-daughter act."

Clarence laughed, a huge annoying hoot.

Emma ignored him.

"What if your ma finds you first?" Teddy asked.

Emma froze. Mother! Was she here now…somewhere at the circus?

"Teddy, will you watch Lucky for me? Stay here till I talk to Filippo?" Emma begged her cousin. "Please?"

"OK," Teddy said. "Can Lucky be my dog if you join the circus?"

She didn't answer him. Lucky would never be anyone's dog but hers.

"You better not run off with the circus," Clarence said.

Emma jumped from the boxcar. She had no time to lose. In a matter of moments Emma would find out if Filippo was her father—if Mother didn't find her first.

# Chapter Thirteen

## Humiliation

At the very moment Emma ran toward Filippo's tent, a cavalcade of menagerie cages rolled toward a line of flatcars that waited on the track. One of the circus trains was pulling out and the matinee hadn't even ended yet. Boss Man had told her this was a "water stop," a one-performance stand. All that work for just one show.

The downpour had ended and the air smelled of mud and wet hay. Roustabouts busily dismantled tents and loaded wagons. Music spilled from the Big Top as Emma ran toward Filippo's tent and quickly ducked into it. Mother would never look for her in the tent.

Emma surveyed the inside, hoping to spot the photograph somewhere, but didn't see it. The tent held a cot, folding chairs, costumes hanging on a clothes rack, water buckets, a trunk with a tray on top that held combs, brushes, a pair of scissors, and, next to it, a long mirror. She caught her reflection in it. Holy cow, was she a sight. Those filthy wet overalls, her hair crammed inside the fedora. She had to do something to improve her looks.

She pulled off the still-damp hat, undid the rubber binder around her hair, and shook her head, running her fingers through the thick curls that framed her face like a lion's mane. Next to the mirror stood the rack of costumes—the prettiest

85

dresses she had ever seen, shiny satin, gold and silver glitter! In one of those costumes, even the most plain-looking girl in the world would look beautiful. Suddenly the idea seized her. Maybe she could find a costume in her size. Something that would make even her look pretty to Filippo. But she had to hurry.

She pulled out a dress with a pink satin bodice bespeckled with a million sequins and a tulle skirt and held it up to her chest. It might fit, but she had to be quick. Any minute Filippo would be there. He couldn't find her half-dressed. Or worse, not dressed at all.

She peeked outside the tent. No performers had entered the backyard yet, but music from the grand finale spilled from the Big Top. After Emma climbed out of her overalls and yanked off her shirt, she caught a glimpse of her reflection and stopped to stare at herself in her underwear. No wonder she had passed so easily for a boy. Her body gave away no hints of womanhood.

*Hurry!* she reminded herself. She slipped the satin and tulle costume off the hanger, and stepped into it, yanking the narrow straps over her shoulder. The bodice fell hopelessly low. She had nothing to fill it with. How ridiculous she looked, her undershirt exposed under the pink satin bodice, her big clodhopper boots sticking out from the flouncy tulle. Frantically she searched the rack for something else. There had to be something she could put on, something that would fit. As she shoved the costumes along the rack, what looked to be a photograph lying on the ground caught her eye. She picked up the photograph—a postcard actually. A lady stared back at her, naked from the waist up, her bosom exposed for all the world to see! Emma had overheard Clarence and his pals talk about these naked lady photos—French postcards they called them. She had to show Nan. She wouldn't believe her eyes. Emma bent down and slipped the postcard into the bib pocket of Clarence's overalls. At that very moment, the tent flap opened and in walked Filippo.

He took one startled look at her and then laughed. "Holy Moses. What the—"

Emma felt her face heat up like an oven. Then, outside the tent door, behind Filippo's back, she saw two figures—a woman in a faded wash dress and a man wearing a white shirt, slacks, and cowboy boots. She couldn't see their faces, but she didn't need to. It was Boss Man and—Mother!

Her heart began beating fast like the wings of a trapped bird.

"Filippo," Boss Man called into the tent, his face still hidden. "A visitor."

Filippo threw Emma a puzzled look, then stepped outside the tent.

"Oh, *mio Dio*," Filippo said. "Sapphira!"

Emma dropped to the ground and scrambled under the cot.

"You're as beautiful as ever." Emma heard Filippo say.

"I didn't come for your flattery. Where's my daughter?"

"Daughter?"

"The girl who came . . . to your tent," Boss Man said. "Do you know where she is?"

"I never saw any *girl*."

"Come on," Boss Man said. "The kid in the overalls."

Filippo laughed. "That filthy kid was a girl? Sapphira's girl? You've got to be joking."

From under the cot, Emma realized Filippo was trying to protect her.. But, she had to escape . . . now.

Crawling on her belly, she lifted the tent bottom and stuck her head out, praying no one would see her wriggle out from under it. She heard Lucky barking and froze. He raced toward her. When he reached her, he whined and licked her face. Her head was the only part of her body outside the tent. In the next moment she spied cowboy boots. Boss Man.

"Curly," he said, and shook his head.

Emma put her finger to her lips to shush him, then wiggled on her belly from under the tent. But it was too late. Mother and Filippo had walked to the back side of the tent.

"Emma!" Mother said.

Emma, still on her knees, still in the tulle and satin dress, held onto Lucky. She was trapped.

"I can't believe you disobeyed me like this!" Mother said, her voice shaking. "And look at you. What did you think you were doing? Stand up, young lady!"

As Emma started to get up, her left boot caught on the tulle skirt, straining a strap on the satin bodice. She felt it snap. With her right hand, she grabbed hold of the strap and stood, Lucky by her side.

Boss Man put his hand over his mouth and coughed. He was trying not to laugh!

Mother grabbed her. "Why are you wearing that dress?"

At that moment, something snapped inside Emma, like

the strap on her dress. She wrangled away from Mother's grasp. "Stop it! I'm not a baby, Mother!"

"Don't talk to me like that!" Mother lifted her hand and slapped Emma's face. For a moment, nothing existed for Emma except the stinging in her cheek and the fury she felt inside. Her mother *did* hate her. And here was the proof of it.

"You lied to me, Emma. Disobeyed me."

Humiliation and rage surged through Emma until they found a voice. "Yes!" she yelled. "But I had to. I had to find him . . . my father! You wouldn't tell me, so I had to find him for myself." She touched her still stinging cheek.

The color drained from Mother's face. "Emma, you don't know what you're talking about."

"Yes, I do. My father is a circus flyer. I found his photograph in your bureau and saw him on a circus poster. Why didn't you tell me?" Emma swallowed back tears.

Mother looked away from her, far away, to those secret places she wouldn't share with Emma. "You shouldn't have been snooping in my room. It was none of your business!"

"None of my business? My own father is none of my business?" she shouted.

"No. Let it go, Emma. Now come with me." She grabbed Emma's wrist.

Emma shook Mother's hand off. "No! I'm staying till I learn the truth!" She pointed to Filippo. "You're my father, aren't you?"

Filippo stood silent, still as a held breath. Then he smiled. "No, *tesora*, I'm not your father. Though I'd be proud to be."

Emma stared at Filippo and then Mother. "But the picture in your drawer? Isn't that him?" Emma asked, pointing at Filippo.

"No," her mother said.

"Tell her, Sapphira," Boss Man said. "She deserves to know."

"She's a child. My child. And what she deserves to know is up to me. Come, Emma."

"The dress," Filippo said. "She needs to leave the dress. It belongs to the circus."

*I belong to the circus,* Emma thought. And her mother was dragging her from it.

The elephants, Emma's elephants, marched trunk to tail toward the waiting train. People scurried by them, barely stopping to look.

Emma jerked her arm free from her mother's clasp.

"Don't you do that!" Mother snapped.

"I have to take this off!" Emma yelled, flicking her hand at the tulle-skirted dress.

Emma stormed inside the tent, Lucky at her heels. Once inside, she collapsed on the cot. Lucky sat on his haunches and cocked his head as if asking, *What now?* She threw her arms around Lucky and buried her face in his fur. She had to think. But her mind was a jumble. If Filippo wasn't her father, then who was? Boss Man's words, "Tell her," echoed in Emma's brain. Boss Man knew about her father. She would ask him, but when and how? Before she could come up with a plan, Mother poked her head in the tent.

"Let's go, Emma."

"I'm not dressed yet!"

"Well, hurry up! I've work to do…and you're coming with me."

Emma stood, slipped off the dress, pulled on her shirt and stepped into the damp overalls. As she was about to shove her hair back into Granddad's fedora, she spied the shiny silver scissors in the tray. She looked at herself in the mirror and began snipping away at her curls. Never would Mother put them in braids again. Never! When she was finished, she shoved Granddad's fedora on her head and stepped outside the tent feeling lighter.

"Emma!" Mother said when she saw her. "Your hair!" She didn't even notice that she was dressed in filthy overalls.

Emma didn't say a word. All she could think of was how hard she had worked to earn a ticket to the Big Show to find the man in the photograph, the man Mother wouldn't tell her about, the father that belonged to her! And for what?

Mother took Emma's hand, but she shook it free, lagging behind Mother as she stormed off the circus grounds. All around them the circus was coming down, being tossed onto the train to be carried off to who-knows-where. She thought of Boss Man and Filippo, how they had looked at her, treated her, like they understood, like she was one of them. She thought of the souvenir she had left them, her curls lying on the ground inside Filippo's tent.

The thunderstorm had cooled the air and left puddles in its wake. Emma's boots hit each puddle with a lusty anger, shooting up a spray she hoped splattered her mother's bare legs. Lucky kept pace beside her. So many questions raced through Emma's mind. Who was the man in the photograph? Who was her father? Why wouldn't Mother tell her? That familiar wall of silence rose up between them. Emma felt exhausted by the work, the heat, and all that had happened in the circus backyard. Still she knew she couldn't let tomorrow come without learning the truth about her father.

As they stepped onto 21st Street, Emma turned her head back toward the circus lot to see tents coming down, wagons loaded, animals gone.

Panic gripped her. How long before every part of the circus would be disassembled and packed onto the trains? How long before Boss Man would be gone along with her chance to find out about her father?

She couldn't let that happen.

She wouldn't.

# CHAPTER FOURTEEN

## A DANGEROUS PLAN

By the time Emma and Mother reached the back door of Dr. Rose's house overlooking Lake Michigan, Emma's anger had transformed into something else. She looked at Mother just ahead of her in her old wash dress now speckled with flecks of mud and promised herself that she would never end up like Mother, hands smelling of bleach, cleaning other people's toilets and washing their underwear. Never! Someday she would be a circus star. She would learn to fly, fly like Filippo the Flying Wonder. She would wear pretty costumes that shone and glittered, dazzle folks with pirouettes and somersaults high above the sawdust, high above the ordinary folk. Everyday Emma would be doing what she loved.

Mother started to open the screen door. Without turning around, she said, "Lucky will have to stay outside, but you come in with me."

"Mother," Emma pleaded. "Can't I stay outside with Lucky?"

Mother's shoulders drooped, her hand gripping the door handle. As always, the ties on her apron hung limply. "Please?" Emma said in a nicer voice this time.

Dr. Rose appeared behind the screen just inside the door. "Emma," he said, pushing his glasses back onto his nose. "You had your mother very worried."

"She worries too much," Emma said.

"That's what mothers do, my child." As he looked her over, his kind, blue eyes nearly twinkled. "And you have a new hairdo. It suits you. Those overalls, too. I think more girls should sport them." He glanced at Mother. "Why don't you let her play in the backyard with Lucky, Sapphira?"

"Because she can't be trusted."

"Now, Sapphira. Can't you let the girl have some space?"

Was Dr. Rose really on her side, or did he not want her inside his house as filthy as she was? She probably smelled like elephant dung, or worse.

Mother looked at her with tired, sad eyes. Emma could still feel the sting of Mother's slap on her cheek. "Well, all right," Mother said. "But stay in the backyard. You've caused enough trouble for one day."

"Can't Lucky and me go down to the lake?"

Mother let out a huge sigh. "Lucky and I. No. Stay in the yard where I can keep an eye on you. Dr. Rose's guests will be coming soon. I've still more food to prepare. I'll be watching from the kitchen. No more shenanigans, young lady."

As Mother stepped inside, Dr. Rose lay his hand on Mother's shoulder and whispered something in her ear. Grown-ups and their secrets. Emma was sick of it. She had to get back to the circus lot and find Boss Man and uncover the one secret Mother insisted on keeping from her. She would stay in the backyard all right, the circus backyard!

Emma picked up a stick and threw it toward the lake. Lucky ran across the wide lawn to catch it. She had to think of a plan that would get her back to the circus grounds and find Boss Man.

She glanced back toward the house. Mother stared out the kitchen window. How could Emma escape this time? If she ran, Mother would be after her in a flash.

Lucky came loping back to her. Just as he dropped the stick at her feet, Clarence's and Teddy's heads appeared over the bluff that led down to the lake.

"Emma!" Teddy shouted. Her cousins scrambled across the lawn toward her.

"What are you doing here?" Clarence asked. "I thought you were going to join the circus," he said in his usual mocking tone. "Your ma find you and drag you here? What happened to your hair? Don't you look swell!"

"Shut up."

"So, what you gonna do now?" Teddy asked.

Emma glanced at Clarence dressed in knickers and a cap. In an instant, a plan of escape formed in her brain. She grabbed Clarence's arm. "Swap clothes with me!"

"What?"

"Please. You've got to. Mother's keeping an eye on me from the window. But I've got to get back to the circus grounds."

"Why?" Teddy asked. "Are you going to run away . . . for real this time?"

"I've got to talk to Boss Man. Clarence, if we swap clothes—you put on these overalls and fedora and I put on your knickers and cap—Mother will think I'm you and you're me. We're nearly the same size. And now that I've short hair…"

"You're crazy, Emma," Clarence said. "When are you going to grow up? Besides, I've outgrown those overalls and why should I help you anyway? I'd only get in a heap of trouble with your mama."

"Because I've got something you want."

"Yeah, like what?" Clarence asked.

"A French postcard."

"What's a French postcard?" Teddy asked.

"A postcard with naked ladies," Emma told him. "I've got one in my pocket."

"Like heck you do," Clarence said.

Emma pulled out the postcard for Clarence to peek at. He blushed a good one before she could shove it back in her pocket. "Clarence, you and me are going to go behind those bushes and swap clothes." Emma pointed to a hedge of lilac bushes near the edge of the bluff about fifty feet from the house. "Then you'll pretend to be me." She smiled at Clarence. "For the French postcard."

"Maybe," Clarence said.

"OK, listen and I'll explain again, but we've got to hurry!" She stared into Clarence's eyes to make sure he was paying attention. "Go knock on the back door and when Mother comes, ask her if you and Teddy can go swimming. You know she always lets you…being boys and all…" Emma had to add. "Then we'll go behind the bushes and swap clothes."

"I ain't undressing in front of you," Clarence protested.

"We'll have our backs to each other and pass the clothes that way," Emma said. "After you're wearing these overalls with the French postcard in the pocket, and I'm wearing your knickers and cap, I'll disappear down the bluff with Lucky and you'll stay in the yard with Teddy."

"Won't she wonder why Teddy didn't go with me?"

"Maybe, but I don't want Teddy going down to the lake by himself. Sorry, Teddy."

"But the clothes you're wearing stink! PU!" Clarence, the BO boy, said. "You're going to have to do something to make this up to me, more than just a French postcard. I'm going to be in a heap of trouble with Aunt Saffy because of you."

"I'll do your chores for a week."

"A month," Clarence insisted.

"OK, a month. So, you better not run off with the circus."

After Emma and Clarence had exchanged clothes behind the lilac hedge, she raced down the bluff with Lucky, pretending to be Clarence heading to the lake. But instead she headed south toward the circus grounds. "Come on, buddy," she told Lucky. "You're coming with me this time. Whatever happens, wherever I go, you're going with me."

When she spotted the path up the bluff that led to Eleventh Street, she and Lucky climbed the steep, sandy trail. The July sun, making its descent into the west, dipped below a bank of clouds, throwing heat onto her back. She guessed it was after five o'clock by now. What would she find when she reached the circus grounds? All the circus trains couldn't be gone yet. They just couldn't!

As she reached the top of the trail, she spotted a bicycle several houses down, leaning up against the Swensen's picket fence. Emma looked toward the porch and the front door. No one in sight. "Shall we borrow this?" she asked Lucky. "It will get us there faster."

Lucky barked twice.

She cruised down Wisconsin Avenue, reveling in the speed until she spotted Mrs. Brosky sitting on her front porch decorated in red, white, and blue bunting for the Fourth.

Mrs. Brosky waved at her. "Hi, Clarence! Happy Fourth! Tell your aunt I wish her the same."

"I will. And happy Fourth to you, too!"

Lucky barked his own greeting.

Holy cow, but fooling people was easy. Was it this simple for everyone, or did she have a natural talent for it? She could see where it would come in handy in life...it already had. By making people think she was someone or something she wasn't, she'd been able to get what she wanted—well, almost. Now what she wanted most of all was the truth and to be her own true self. She pedaled hard, frantic that she wouldn't find Boss Man before he left.

When Emma rode close enough to catch a glimpse of the circus lot, the sight before her nearly made her lose her balance and tumble onto the street. The Big Top convulsed to the earth like a gigantic dying moth. Roustabouts threw themselves at the canvas, grabbing at it, trying to speed its demise.

She pedaled quickly across the field, her feet and heart pumping fast, praying that Boss Man would still be there.

# Chapter Fifteen

## Secrets Revealed

As Emma pedaled across the circus lot, feathery clouds drifted in front of the sun that hovered low on the horizon. Dozens of men swarmed over the fallen Big Top, unlacing and rolling the flattened canvas. Wagons rumbled toward the railroad crossing where the flatcars waited. Animals screeched and roared from inside cages that were being rolled and jostled toward the waiting train.

Where could Boss Man be? Emma's sweaty undershirt and underpants stuck to her skin; her feet ached in their too-small boots. She felt exhausted, but she couldn't quit now.

"Scram, kid," a roustabout shouted at her. "A tear down ain't no place for rubes...or their dogs."

All around her, men rolled the Big Top into huge bundles and began hoisting them onto trucks. A tall black man, with huge muscles glanced over his shoulders at her.

"I'm looking for the boss," Emma said.

"Ain't seen 'im," the roustabout replied.

She pedaled toward the section of the circus lot where Filippo's tent had been. Workers scurried about loading huge wooden trunks onto wagons.

And then she saw him. Filippo, dressed in cuffed white slacks and a dark blue shirt, his hair slicked back and looking for all the world like some sort of movie star. Her heart beat fast. She called to him.

He turned and started walking toward her. "You again?" he said, grinning at her. "Don't you know how to dress like a girl? And your hair." He shook his head. "*Tsk, tsk, tsk.* I guess you're here because you want those curls back…or maybe you want to run away with the circus." He smiled at her like people do when they're half-joking. His two front teeth, Emma couldn't help noticing, overlapped slightly the way hers did. And he had dark eyes framed by thick lashes and a dimple on his chin—the same as the man in the photograph. He had to be her father. Why couldn't he say so?

"I came to talk to the circus boss."

He bent down to scratch Lucky behind both ears. Lucky's tail wagged gratefully. "Fine dog you've got here. Used to have a setter." He stood and lit a stub of a cigarette. "So why don't you want to join the circus like your mama?"

"What?"

"If you're half as good as your mama was, I could make you a star," he said. "You look surprised, *tesora.*"

*Mother? In the circus…?* A chill skittered down Emma's spine. *The feathered headband in the box with the photo!* It had been Mother's! Mother had been in the circus—it seemed impossible, but here it was …the truth, the impossible, astounding truth. And Filippo *had* to be her father, but why wouldn't he say so?

"Tell me. Tell me the truth! You lied this afternoon, didn't you? You *are* my father, aren't you?" She was shaking now.

Emma felt a hand on her shoulder. Someone stood behind her. She recognized the cologne. Boss Man.

100

"Come with me, Emma."

*Who is my father?* Emma wanted to shout the question, but she was too shocked by Boss Man's strong grip on her arm, leading her away from Filippo…to where? She soon got her answer as Boss Man led her across the back lot to a railroad car, a Pullman car with windows. A crow pecked at something on the ground near the railroad car and flew off as they approached.

"Go ahead," Boss Man said. "Climb aboard."

"Why?" she asked.

"You'll see. Tell your dog to stay."

"Stay, Lucky. I'll be right back."

Lucky stared at her with his large brown eyes and let out a small whine.

"I'm OK," she said. "I'll be right back. Stay."

Inside the railroad car it was too dark to see much of anything, but the air felt damp and smelled musty. When her eyes had adjusted to the dim light, she saw men's clothes on a hook, a pair of cowboy boots on the floor with a cowboy hat perched on top. She guessed this small room in the railroad car belonged to Boss Man. But why had he taken her here?

"Sit down," he said, pointing to a narrow bunk.

She sat, while Boss Man reached up onto a shelf and pulled out a leather book the size of Nan's scrapbook, the one filled with movie star photographs. He moved the single chair in the room in front of her and eased into it, flipping through the pages.

What was he looking for?

"Here," he said, handing Emma a photograph that had

been tucked between the pages. Boss Man switched on a lamp that sat on a small desk littered with papers.

Emma stared at the photograph. A young woman and young man sat together on a trapeze. She was wearing a feathered headband like the one hidden in Mother's bureau. The girl, without a doubt, was a younger version of Mother and the young man was…Filippo. Emma's eyes stung with tears. "So Filippo *is* my father. Why couldn't he tell me?"

"That boy is your father, Emma. But he's not Filippo."

"What? You're lying! That has to be Filippo!" She was so sick of all the lying, the secrets. All she wanted was the truth. Why wouldn't anyone tell her the truth?

"That's Paolo, Filippo's brother. Do you understand what I'm saying?"

Boss Man sat quiet for a moment as if to give her time to let his words sink in. "He and Sapphira…your mama…were in love. They had an adorable baby—you."

Emma stared at the girl in the photograph, so happy, so young. At the movies, she'd seen girls in love. The girl's face in the photograph, her own mother's face, looked like those girls. And the young man? Did he love her back? And where was he now, her father, the man in the photograph?

"So, where is he? This man…my…father?" The words sounded strange to her ears.

Boss Man placed his hand over hers. It felt warm and leathery. "Gone, Emma. Dead."

"Dead?" she felt the blood drain from her face.

"A circus accident. He was trying a new stunt. He asked for the net to be rolled back that night—"

"How could there *not* be a net?" she shouted.

"It was Paolo's decision…to sell more tickets."

She stared at the man in the photograph again—her very own father—doing something so stupid, so risky, so horrible that it caused his own death. How could he? And then she remembered the Kinzie River Bridge railing.

"This scrapbook belonged to your mama. I put the photograph of Paolo you showed me in it, too. Why don't you take it to her?"

"I can't." Emma put her head in her hands. "Mother didn't want me to know, but now I do. I can't go home. Please let me stay here…with the circus." She sat up and looked at Boss Man. "Let me have a chance. Please? I'm good at acrobatics. Filippo can teach me to fly. I learn fast. And you know I work hard." She found the courage to look at Boss Man at last. And he looked at her…with that same look Granddad sometimes had, eyes soft, mouth hard.

Boss Man shook his head, his hand still on hers. "No. I've no doubt you could be anything you set your mind to be. But—"

"No! I can't go home."

"You belong with your mama and when you grow up—"

"Grow up? I am grown up!" As she said those words, she could feel herself wanting to sob like a baby. She was so tired, tired of fighting for every inch, and people pushing her back a mile. But she wouldn't give in. She wasn't a baby.

"Go home, Emma. Go home."

Emma bent over and buried her face in her hands.

"Emma, I know this all comes as an awful shock to you.

103

I'm sorry. I really am. But the truth of the matter is that your mama loves you more than you know. She could have given you up for strangers to raise or brought you back to the circus, but chose to go home to her father to bring you up proper. She never had a mama herself but wanted you to have one."

This was all news to Emma. She never thought about why they lived with Granddad, about him not having a wife or her not having a Grandmother.

"Your arrival in this world, Emma, changed everything."

*Changed everything.*

The whistle on the train sounded.

"The five-minute whistle," Boss Man said. "You've got to go, Emma."

She didn't move. She couldn't. Boss Man leaned over and wrapped his arms around her. They felt like Granddad's and tears stung her eyes.

Then, as if she were two years old, Boss Man lifted her up and carried her off the train.

When her feet touched the ground, she wondered if her legs would hold her.

"You're gonna be fine. And come next summer, if you feel the same way about the circus and you get your mama's blessing…well, we'll see."

Steam began hissing from the engine and the whistle sounded again. Emma threw her arms around Boss Man. When she finally let go, he handed her the scrapbook. "Take this."

Emma grasped the book, then turned around and ran, Lucky beside her.

# CHAPTER SIXTEEN

## NOW WHAT?

Emma found the bicycle and her boots where she had left them on the circus lot. She set the boots and the leather-bound scrapbook in the basket.

Now what? She watched the last circus train slowly disappear, heading south to the next town and the next show. With the back of her hand she brushed the tears off her cheeks. Boss Man had been so kind to her, so honest, more than Mother had been, and Filippo, was her very own uncle, a famous circus star. She couldn't bear to think of them vanishing from her life, maybe for forever.

The sun had sunk low in the west and folks in Model-Ts, horse-drawn wagons, and on foot were heading to the lakeshore for the fireworks. Emma pedaled a block and stopped. She had to think. She leaned the bicycle against a bench at the edge of the bluff overlooking the lake and collapsed onto it. Lucky rested his head on her knees and stared up at her. "What am I going to do, Lucky?" she said, rubbing her hand across his soft fur.

The water that earlier had churned up white-capped waves was calm now. Only a few clouds lingered over the lake. The huge dome of the sky glowed a dusky blue, and the nearly full moon rose in the east. She thought about Boss Man and all that he had told her. It seemed like a dream. The whole day an illusion, some strange trick of her imagination. Still, Boss Man's words echoed in her mind. Everything now started to make sense—why Mother didn't want to talk about her father, why she had so easily learned to do cartwheels and back flips when the other kids struggled, why seeing the circus parade filled her with such longing. She was the daughter of circus people. The circus *was* in her blood. But would Mother let her do what she had been born to do? Next July when the circus came to Racine would Boss Man let Filippo—her very own uncle—train her?

Mother! What would she do when she discovered Emma was missing this time? The thought made her scalp prickle and her stomach knot. She couldn't bear another slap across the face. Still, she imagined she was in store for something far worse now. How could she face her mother ever again?

Unable to move, not knowing what to do, she sat watching the lake change color as the sun set, from burnt orange, to purple, to gray. She bent down to pick up a stone, so smooth and polished it shone. As she cupped her fingers around it, pressing it against her palm, something in the stone's slippery coolness calmed her. Yes, her day had been a long string of lies and deceptions; still, in the end she had learned the truth. Had she the chance, would she have done things differently? No, she was glad she'd done what she had, for now she knew who she was and what she wanted. She drew back her arm and threw the stone as far as she could toward the water, then hopped back on the borrowed bicycle. "Come on, Lucky. Let's go!" She pushed her bare feet hard against the pedals, suddenly no longer tired but filled with a fierce determination to set things right.

As she pedaled down Wisconsin Avenue, the streetlights flickered on. About half a block away, she spotted a boy running toward her.

"Hey, my bicycle!" he yelled. "*You* stole it!"

"I only borrowed it."

"Yeah, right!" He grabbed the handle bar and jerked it hard. "Give me my bike."

Emma lost her balance and tumbled to the gutter, the bicycle with her. Her boots and the leather scrapbook sailed from the basket onto the wet street.

"Hey, you're a girl," the boy sneered. "What happened to your hair? Did it get caught in a combine?"

Emma ignored his comment. She reached for the scrapbook lying near the rain-filled gutter. The boy got to it first. "What's this?" he asked, picking up the brown leather book, its cover streaked with water.

A motor car rumbled by. A kid in the back seat hung his head out the window, staring at them.

"None of your business!" Emma shouted. She tried to grab the book from him, but he jerked it away. "Give me that!" she said. Lucky growled low in his throat.

The boy flipped through the pages of photos and news clippings, holding it out of her reach. A fury rose in Emma and she pounced on him like a wild animal. She landed so hard he lost his balance and fell onto the grass between the street and the sidewalk. Emma pounded him with her fists. Lucky clamped his teeth on the boy's pant leg. Another motor car passed and honked at them.

"Oww! That hurts," the boy whined. "Stop it! I'm not going to fight a girl, even if she is dressed like a boy. You can have your dumb book, you dirty little tomboy!"

Emma got up and grabbed the book out of the gutter, then looked over at the boy who slowly sat up.

"Come on, Lucky." Emma marched down the sidewalk, the scrapbook and boots in hand. A more important battle lay ahead.

# Chapter Seventeen

## "It's All Your Fault"

Dr. Rose's backyard glowed with paper lanterns strung from trees. Some kids raced around waving sparklers. A few others were playing Simon Says. Grown-ups stood in clumps chatting, or lounged in the dozens of chairs that dotted the wide lawn overlooking the lake. The soft evening air echoed with laughter and conversation, as if this were any ordinary Fourth of July. Soon the fireworks would start—and not just, Emma feared, the ones exploding in the sky.

Emma surveyed the crowded backyard but didn't see Mother.

Again, she felt the slap across her cheek and recalled the look on Mother's face outside Filippo's tent. Now that she thought about it, that look was more than just one of anger—Emma had seen Mother angry before. The expression on Mother's face had been more like...what? Fear? And now Emma knew why.

As Emma waited, unseen, near the edge of the yard, a mosquito landed on her arm. She smacked it. How easy it was to kill a mosquito, but not before it left you with an itch you scratched till it got bloody. Emma scratched her arm and reached down to pet Lucky. Whatever happened, she would have Lucky. That thought gave her comfort and courage. Still, what was she going to say to Mother...and

Mother to her…now that Emma had learned the truth, the truth Mother had tried so hard to keep from her?

As Emma started toward the lantern-lit lawn, a crow swooped from a tree and glided onto the grass a few feet in front of her, cocking its head toward her. She recalled the crow yesterday morning outside Brosky's window where she had seen the poster, and the one that landed in front of Boss Man's Pullman car. She clutched the scrapbook closer and stepped out of the shadows into the light. The crow flew off.

Nan spotted her first. "Emma!" she said, running to her.

"Look! It's Emma!" Teddy called. "We thought you'd ran off with the circus for sure. I told everybody you did! Why didn't you?"

"What happened to your hair?" Nan said. "Oh, my gosh! Emma!" Nan's hand flew to her mouth.

Emma shook her head.

Kids, most of whom she didn't know, gathered around her, petting Lucky. Grown-ups, who milled on the lawn holding plates of food and chatting, seemed not to notice her arrival. She still didn't see Mother among them. Where was she?

"Did you find your father?" Nan asked, putting her arm around Emma's waist and scooting her away from the crowd. "What's that?" She pointed at the scrapbook.

Emma didn't want to talk, not even to Nan. She felt so tired, like she could lie down right there on the grass and sleep for a million years.

"Here, sit down on our blanket," Nan said. "I want to hear everything…when you're ready."

"Are you hungry?" a little girl in a white pinafore asked. "Here, you can have mine." She held out a plate.

Emma stared at the hot dog with its stripe of yellow mustard and the wedge of watermelon and her mouth began to water. "Thanks," she told the girl, smiling up at her. Until that moment, Emma hadn't realized how long it had been since she had eaten the lunch Nan had brought her.

"How come you're dressed like a boy?" the pinafored girl asked sweetly. "Teddy told us you can do circus tricks. Will you show us please...when you finish eating?"

"She's tired," Nan said. "Let her alone."

Emma broke off a piece of hot dog and held it out to Lucky. He devoured it in one gulp. Emma bit down on hers. It popped in her mouth, the salty juices bursting over her tongue. If only she could enjoy it.

"Here," a blond-headed boy said, handing her a glass of lemonade.

Several kids hovered around her as she ate, staring at her like she was some sort of sideshow freak. Pinafore girl lolled next to her on the blanket, her arm draped over Lucky.

"So, how come you didn't join the circus?" the blond boy asked.

"Emma!" Clarence yelled, shoving his way through the kids. "Your ma's sick, and you're in a heap of trouble!"

Emma felt the hot dog and lemonade rise in her throat.

"She thought you'd run away with the circus," Clarence said. "You're mean and selfish, Emma. I should never have helped you."

"Emma's not mean!" Nan said. "She was just trying to

find her father!"

The kids stood around gawking at her.

"Where is she?" Emma asked.

"In the house, on the sofa, sick. It's all your fault!"

Mother never got sick.

Nan took Emma's hand.

"Granddad's with your ma, and Dr. Rose and some men went over to the circus lot to try and find you!" Clarence said. "Your ma may be dying and it's all your fault."

"You're lying!"

"Yeah, well go and see for yourself. Get in there, Emma," Clarence said, pointing to the house. "You need to try to set things right…for a change."

Emma jumped up from the blanket. "Shut up! What do you know about setting things right?"

The kids who had swarmed around her earlier had run off to play. Even Teddy had abandoned her now that it seemed she wasn't going to do acrobatics for them.

"Want me to go with you?" Nan asked.

Emma shook her head. "Watch Lucky, OK? Don't go home."

Emma shoved Clarence out of her way as she stormed toward the back door. Her legs shook and she felt like she was going to throw up, but she held up her chin. She wasn't going to show Clarence she was afraid, a kind of fear she hadn't felt before. What had she done?

Dr. Rose's brightly lit kitchen sat empty and silent. She could hear talking and laughter coming from the backyard. She looked toward the hall that led to the front door. The living room stood at the front of the house at the far end of the hallway on the left. She stepped slowly toward it into the long, wide hall, several doors on either side, her stomach tied in a million knots.

When she was halfway down the hall, the windowed doors to the living room opened and out stepped Granddad, staring at the floor, his shoulders sagging. At that moment Emma knew something was terribly wrong.

And then he saw her.

"Emma! Oh, thank God! Thank God."

Tears stung her eyes.

"Mother…how is Mother?" She hurried toward him, stopping just before she reached him.

Granddad lifted his spectacles and wiped his forehead with his handkerchief. His bow tie—red, white, and blue for the Fourth—bent cock-eyed. "Step in here, Emma." He motioned to a room across the hall from the living room. A single lamp on a large desk lit the room that smelled faintly of antiseptic. Books filled an entire wall. "Sit down," he said, pointing to a small leather sofa. She dropped into it. Granddad sat next to her.

"Mother's dying, isn't she? And it's all my fault!" The words burst from her. The most horrible words she could ever utter, strung together to make one unimaginable thought. People died—Aunt Grace, the father she never even got to know, and now Mother. She buried her face in her hands.

Granddad slid close to her and put his arm around her. He felt warm and smelled of perspiration, cigar smoke and Fels Naptha soap. "Emma, no. Of course not. Your mother's ill from fatigue and worry. But she's alive as can be. Dr. Rose gave her some medicine that makes people sleepy. She's sleeping now. And, now that you're safe . . . well, everything will be fine." He stroked her hair. "She told me you had cut it," Granddad said. "Your beautiful hair."

Relief rippled through Emma. She couldn't care less about her hair. Mother was *not* dying. Mother was *not* dying!

Emma sobbed so hard she shook. Her nose ran with snot. Granddad handed her his handkerchief and she blew and blew some more. Granddad continued to hold her until her gasps stopped and she breathed slow and even. She concentrated on her breath, and the smell of leather, and the smell of soap, and the smell of sweat and cigar, and the warmth and weight of Granddad's arm on her, and the sound of breathing, in and out, in and out. She was alive and Mother was not dying, and Emma had not killed her. And everything was going to be fine. But Emma knew...no, it was not. Not until...

"Emma?" Granddad's voice was soft. "We need to talk about something. And then you can see your mother."

Emma's heart skipped a beat. Her head still bent, she opened her eyes that felt all puffy and stared at her hands, one clutching Granddad's damp handkerchief, the other the scrapbook resting on her lap.

"What's this?" Granddad asked, tapping his fingers on the scrapbook.

"The circus boss gave it to me. It belonged to Mother."

"May I look?"

"Should you ask Mother? Maybe?"

"You're right," Granddad said. "Oh, child. I wish you knew how much anguish you have caused your mother." Emma thought she did know.

Granddad lifted his arm from her and sat up. "When she thought you had run away with the circus…well, let's just say I've never seen her so distraught and your mother is a very strong woman. Look how she takes care of Dr. Rose's house and ours. How she cared for your Aunt Grace when she was ill, taking in Clarence and Teddy when she died and their father lost his farm. Doing laundry to make ends meet. She is an amazing woman, Emma. I hope you appreciate that."

Emma knew about the things Mother did, but had never thought much about them. Mother was just Mother, so often tired and crabby. But every evening when Emma came home, she was there. She cooked their dinners and washed their clothes, signed their school papers, and had conferences with their teachers. Mother, who sewed Emma's clothes and braided her hair, who kept house for Dr. Rose and took in other people's laundry, other people's thrown-away kids, and dogs. Mother who gave up a life in the circus because… because she had a baby and that baby was her.

Emma said nothing, just kept staring at her hands on the scrapbook, counting the knuckles—*one, two, three, four, five, six, seven, eight—who do you appreciate?* The silly jump rope rhyme. The mosquito bite on her arm started itching like crazy. *Scratch. Scratch. Scratch.* She watched the blood ooze. Could people die from mosquito bites?

"Come," Granddad said, patting her leg. "When your mother wakes up, yours will be the first face she'll want to see. Want to go and wash up at bit?" He smiled, his blue eyes twinkling behind his glasses.

Emma nodded.

When Emma finally walked into Dr. Rose's living room with Granddad next to her, the first thing she noticed was how peaceful Mother looked, how beautiful, lying there on the sofa—like Sleeping Beauty. Emma stared at her, searching for the girl in the scrapbook pictures, the young girl on the flying trapeze. What had become of her? She was gone, of course. Dead. Clarence was right after all. Emma *had* killed her. By Emma simply being born, Sapphira, the happy girl on the flying trapeze, had died just as certainly as if she had fallen from a trapeze. And she didn't go to heaven either. You couldn't call taking care of a bratty tomboy like Emma, heaven. Or doing other folks' laundry, cleaning other folks' houses, taking care of other folks' kids and thrown-away dogs.

Even though the room was hot and sticky, Emma started to tremble. What was going to happen when Mother opened her eyes and saw her—dirty, sweaty, and now wearing Clarence's knickers? Emma clutched the scrapbook tight and waited.

# CHAPTER EIGHTEEN

## TRUTH

The grandfather clock near the living room door chimed nine times. Mother still hadn't opened her eyes. Granddad slipped his arm over Emma's shoulder and kissed the top of her head, then pulled a chair close to the sofa. "Here. Sit down. Did you want to wake her?"

Emma shook her head. She wasn't ready, not yet. "Are you sure she's going to be OK? She looks so pale and she's hardly breathing." She wished she could put a mirror under Mother's nose and see a white cloud appear. Then she would know...know she was still alive.

"Emma, believe me. When she sees your face, she will be more than OK." There was a smile in his voice. "I'll leave you alone with your mother. Besides, the fireworks will be starting soon." He winked at her.

Granddad laid his hand gently on Emma's shoulder and left the room.

She opened the scrapbook to the first page.

*Council Bluffs, Iowa. 1917. Rain didn't stop us!*

A photograph of Mother holding an umbrella, while a young man—Paolo...Emma's father—carried Mother piggy back over a muddy field. Both were smiling, both dressed in costumes for their trapeze act. Mother wearing the headband with the feather, the one Emma had found in the box in Mother's bureau. Emma wondered who took the photograph. Maybe Filippo. Maybe Boss Man. She couldn't take her eyes off Paolo. Her father! What would he have thought of her? Would he have taught her to fly? Would he have loved her? *To my sweet baby girl, with all my love, Papa*—the writing on the photo had said.

A big, black fly buzzed inside a lampshade. The grandfather clock ticked off the seconds. Fireworks sounded over the lake. Emma slowly turned the pages of the scrapbook studying the faces—clowns, acrobats, bareback riders. They all looked so joyful, so proud—like they were one big, happy family. So why didn't Mother stay? But Emma knew the answer—because of her, that's why.

When Emma turned to the last page, she couldn't help but smile—a newspaper clipping of Tina the Fat Lady in her satin rompers, white anklets with lace trim, and ballet slippers. Next to her stood Boss Man sporting his white cowboy hat. She felt a hollow spot in her stomach thinking she may never see him again. Still, now when she thought about it, how much more she would have missed Mother and Granddad had he let her go with him. She closed the scrapbook and set it on the side table.

Emma stared at Mother, lying so still, her beautiful auburn hair cascading over the pillow. She reached closer to feel its silkiness between her fingers. Then she gently touched Mother's cheek, and then her own cheek, the place where Mother had slapped it. She had deserved it.

"I'm sorry, Mother." Emma said the words fast, like she *had* to say them quickly or maybe she might not be able to say them at all.

An explosion of fireworks over the lake shook the windows.

Mother's eyes opened. "Emma?" she whispered. She tried to sit up, but collapsed back onto the pillow. "You're safe. Thank God." Mother shut her eyes again. Tears leaked from the corners and slipped onto the pillowcase.

"I'm sorry," Emma said, easier this time.

"You didn't run away with the circus."

"No. I just had to find out...about my father."

"And you did?"

"Yes."

Silence. The fly buzzed again, banging stupidly against the inside of the lampshade.

"I should have told you, but—"

"I know. Boss Man told me everything."

"It should have been me." Mother took Emma's hand.

"It doesn't matter now," Emma said. And it didn't.

"You were so beautiful. I loved you instantly." Mother smiled. "I named you after my mother who died when I was only ten. I wanted you to be like her, kind and good. Not like me, wild and selfish, running away to join the circus."

*Love.* The word leaped out from all the others and danced around Emma's heart. Mother loved her...but that was when she was a baby! Babies are easy to love. They have no mistakes in them yet. What about when they're older? Did Mother love her now with all her mistakes? She wasn't kind or good. She was wild and selfish and...

Mother shook her head and took both Emma's hands.

"Emma, you have my mother's name, but…" She gazed into Emma's eyes as if she could see into her heart. "When I look at you, I see myself and I'm…afraid."

"Why?"

"I don't want your life to turn out like mine."

"Sapphira," Granddad stood in the doorway, smiling. "You're awake."

Mother turned to look at him. "Emma's come home."

"I know," Granddad said.

Granddad sank into the sofa next to Mother and slipped his arm over her shoulders. "How do you feel?"

Mother squeezed Emma's hand softly. "Honestly? Something like I've just finished a high-flying act and I'm standing on the ground, alive." She smiled at Emma.

"And you?" Granddad asked Emma.

Emma stared at Mother and Granddad and shrugged. She didn't know how she felt, confused mostly. Did Mother love her still, now that she was no longer a baby with no mistakes?

Granddad lifted his arm from Mother's shoulder and held her hand, the one Emma wasn't holding. He took Emma's other hand. She and Granddad and Mother were a little circle connected by hands. She swallowed a giggle thinking of the three of them getting up and playing Ring Around the Rosie—Dr. Rosie. And then she did start giggling. She couldn't help it.

Mother smiled. "What's so funny?"

Emma didn't know, but suddenly everything seemed hilarious. The fly buzzing like mad inside the lampshade; Granddad's red, white, and blue bowtie all crooked, the smeared lenses of his glasses; Mother's bare feet. She thought of the photograph of Tina in her silly rompers and Boss Man in his cowboy hat, how she thought she had fooled them; the elephants snatching Granddad's fedora and spraying her with water; how she peed on the circus grounds; the clowns kidnapping her and making her part of their act; the circus costume she had tried to wear, and the strap that broke; cutting off her hair; the French postcard with the bare-bosomed lady; and Filippo, who she thought was her father. Emma laughed until tears streamed down her cheeks. Everything in the whole world was so hilariously funny, one big clown act!

When she finally stopped laughing, Mother and Granddad were staring at her with strange looks on their faces. But this time Emma didn't laugh, even though Mother and Granddad looked so silly. They both kept holding Emma's hands, tight. More fireworks exploded over the lake.

"I have something I need to tell you," Emma said. She swallowed and brushed an imaginary crumb off her knickers. "I'd like to be a flyer...like you were, Mother, in the circus."

Mother and Granddad looked at each other. They said nothing.

"Someday," Emma added.

Mother sighed and her shoulders relaxed.

"And next summer when the circus comes to town, I want us all to go," Emma said.

"Sapphira?" Granddad said.

"Oh, please, Mother! I want Granddad to meet Boss Man and Filippo . . . my uncle," Emma said. "No more secrets."

Mother looked into Emma's eyes, squeezed her hand and smiled, *I love you.* Emma squeezed Mother's hand back, then Granddad's. *I love you.*

They were still a circle connected by hands. No one had let go.

Emma heard noises at the window and turned to look. Teddy had his nose and mouth pressed against the window making a hideous-looking face squished on the glass. Behind him gawked Clarence and Nan. Lucky, on his haunches, scratched at the window.

"What a bunch of Nosey Nells!" Emma said.

But when Nan waved and her cousin Clarence smiled and Teddy did a goofy dance, she suddenly felt light and giddy, as if she had let go of a trapeze and was sailing through the air.

She felt the hands that would catch her when she fell.

CPSIA information can be obtained
at www.ICGtesting.com
Printed in the USA
FFHW021941211218
49952296-54611FF